Cloud Skimmers

June Whatley

Copyright © 2021 by June Whatley

Published by Jurnee Books, an imprint of Winged Publications

This book is a work of fiction. Names, characters, places, and incidents are the product of the author's imagination and are used fictitiously. Any resemblance to actual events, locales, or persons, living or dead, is coincidental.

All rights reserved including the right to reproduce this book or portions thereof in any form whatsoever – except short passages for reviews – without express permission.

ISBN: 978-1-952661-62-4

Dedication

This book is dedicated to
six of my best friends in the world.

Josiah, Emily, Zion, Miriam,
and
Bear, and Millie.

Outline

Chapter 1 Not Like He'd Planned	Page 1
Chapter 2 Petroglyphs	Page 17
Chapter 3 What You Seek	Page 29
Chapter 4 Bones of the Giants	Page 34
Chapter 5 Travel Plans	Page 46
Chapter 6 The Rebellion	Page 58
Chapter 7 Fallen Ones	Page 65
Chapter 8 Water	Page 69
Chapter 9 More Water!	Page 80
Chapter 10 Og of Bashan	Page 84
Chapter 11 Into the Sun	Page 88
Chapter 12 Which Way In?	Page 101
Chapter 13 The Tower	Page 112
Chapter 14 The Shock	Page 126
Chapter 15 The Fourth Industrial Revolution	Page 133
Chapter 16 Comfort	Page 141

Acknowledgements

"I must express my appreciation to Dr. Thomas Horn of Skywatch TV and to Steve Quayle of GenSix Productions for the inspiration to write this book. I believe their information on giants, transhumanism, A.I. and aliens is crucial to pass on to our young people today."

Hello and a big thank you to my Beta Readers for *Cloud Skimmers.*
A hardy "Thank You!" to Ana Ruth G., Tiffany G., Rebekah G., and Michaela G. from Fairmount, IN.
You are all blessings.

Thanks to my husband who has driven me
all over the country to writers' conferences.
He says he is in
Transportation and Labor.

Chapter 1

Not Like He'd Planned

A plume of yellow dust stirred in the distance, the mica particles of the New Mexico sand reflected the sunlight, the cloud alerted Mican to the approach of a vehicle.

He scurried from his perch on the plateau and arrived, breathless, at the edge of camp. As the jeep stopped, fine powdery dirt billowed into the air, he waved the cloud from his face.

His sister's high-pitched voice erupted from the backseat. "Get your hands off of me, Ashy.

His brother's voice flared back. "Will you get your forty pounds of baggage off of my foot before you cripple me?"

Mican tipped his head back, they rarely argued. Why now? Why here? What had he gotten himself into? Maybe it's just the heat. He forced a smile and stepped to the car to greet his siblings. "Hey you two. How about a 'hello' for your big brother?"

Ashton shoved the door with his foot, forcing Mican aside. "Yeah, right." He pulled himself out.

Shayla stood in the open-topped vehicle; dust collected in the sweat at her temples. She threw her head back and a heavy sigh escaped from her open mouth. "Hey, Mican. Two whole weeks of this? I'm not sure I will survive." She dragged her bags across the vinyl seat and stepped out.

Mican wrapped his arms around her for a hug and lowered his voice. "Shayla, watch what you say. You know your words have power." He straightened, grinned, and announced through clenched teeth. "Watch it, you two. You'd better be on your best behavior, or we could all be sent home. And *I* don't want to go home. Is that understood?"

Ashton's head sloughed to the side. "Yeah, got it."

Mican focused his eyes squarely on his sister. "Shay?"

"I'm sorry, yes, I understand."

At that moment, Dr. Lightfoot strolled up and offered a hearty greeting. "Welcome to Chaco Canyon. Yes, it is pronounced 'Choc-oh,' like chocolate. We are glad to have you on the team. Mican speaks very highly of you. Keep in mind this is a working camp. No lounging around the pool here." He ended with a pleasant chuckle.

They smiled in response, with Ashton adding, "Yes sir, we know. We'll work hard for you."

"That's fine. I will see you after dinner. Mican will show you where to go to get settled." He pushed his hands in his pockets and whistled as he walked away.

With his back to them, their smiles melted, their dimples smoothed into their faces.

Mican watched the camp director walk away before he turned to them and smiled. "I'm glad to see both of you." He leaned in close and whispered in a stern voice. "Make sure it stays that way." He reached for the handle of Shayla's largest bag, she grabbed the two smaller ones, while Ashton lifted his canvas carryall and tossed it over his shoulder.

Then Mican shouted, "Okay troops!"

Ashton's and Shayla's shoulders jerked up when their brother's face tightened, his forehead wrinkled, and he barked out the rest of the order.

"Walk this way." He did a sharp military-type turn, with his back to them, he squatted and waddled like a duck.

Shayla burst out laughing. "I get it. Walk this way. Funny."

Their tall, lanky brother looked so odd, even Ashton chuckled.

After a few awkward waddles, Mican stood straight, placed his hand on his hip and arched. "Oooo, my back." Now only a few feet away from a beige, desert-camo tent, Mican turned to his sister. "Shayla, you will bunk in there with Bailey."

A pretty, young girl about Mican's age, strolled up. "Did I hear my name?"

"Hey Bailey, this is my sister Shayla and our brother Ashton."

Bailey took a bag from Shayla and led the way. "Welcome to Dust City. I hope you aren't allergic to dirt."

Mican pulled the tent flap open wider and motioned both girls inside. Once they were through the entry, he shoved Shayla's big bag in behind them. "See you girls in the mess tent."

***

Half an hour later a dinner triangle beckoned the campers.

Mican waited outside the dining hall.

Bailey exited the tent followed by Shayla. Bailey's long straight hair blew in the wind, unlike his sister's heavy, curly locks that rested on her shoulders and back. They strolled toward him.

"Hey Bailey, thanks for everything, but I'm going to sit with Mican and let him fill me in on what we're supposed to do."

Bailey pushed her hair behind her ear and glanced at him. "That's fine with me, lead the way. He's a hunk and Ash-boat isn't bad either."

Mican dropped his gaze to the sand, until the girls reached him and he looked up to greet his sister.

She rolled her eyes, but held her tongue.

Bailey smiled at him as she glided past.

They went through the serving line and chose from the somewhat recognizable southwestern dishes, then found seats.

Shayla slid in next to her brother and lowered her voice. "Thanks for pairing me with such a nice, *friendly* girl, Bubba."

Mican bent his head, stared into his plate and

chuckled. He glanced back at her and gave a big smile. "My pleasure, Shay."

Bailey scooted in next to her. "Oh, how sweet. Can I call you Shay too?"

Mican placed his hand on his sister's shoulder and grinned. "Sure, you can. She loves it."

Shayla tried to talk with him to get a feel for how things were done at camp, but Bailey insisted. "Oh, you'll figure it out. Don't worry. Let's just get to know each other, I'm Bailey Suzonne Vandenberg. My middle name is pronounced Su-zahn, the 'o' sounds like 'ah,' I hate it when people say Suzanne. And my last name is really supposed to be written in three parts, Van Den Berg, but I think it looks too snooty, so I just write it as one word. My mom gets mad when I sign my school papers like that, but hey, it's my life, right?"

Ashton joined them as Bailey made the disrespectful comment about her mother, taking the seat across from his sister, who glanced at him, reached for the salt and *accidentally* knocked it over toward Bailey. For one millisecond, Bailey stopped talking and Shayla seized the moment. "Sorry, Bailey. Hi, Ashy, how is your tent? Are you getting settled in?"

"Well Shay, it's just like home. I mean, *exactly* like

home. Lucky me, I'm bunking with my big brother."

Shayla babbled on. "Oh, bubba, that is lucky."

But before she could continue, Bailey broke in. "Hey, you can bunk with me and Shay. We'll take you." She laughed, twisted a lock of her hair, and grinned.

Ashton's face turned pink and his gaze fell to his plate. "Well—uhh…."

Mican knew his brother was no match for her, so he sprang to his rescue. "Bailey, I don't think I could sleep a wink knowing that my brother had crowded in on our sister and her new best friend."

"I know what you mean. Shay-girl and I hit it off right away, she's like, you know, like just the best ever."

An all-too-one-sided conversation dominated the rest of the meal, until a staff member announced the evening activity.

The group gathered at the center of camp, where the staffer built a fire and all of the campers settled.

The young, tanned camp director, Dr. Jerome Lightfoot, stood and fastened his eyes on Bailey. "I'm sure we will all listen respectfully to our guests tonight."

Seated on the ground, leaning back on her straightened arms, Bailey rolled her eyes.

Dr. Lightfoot introduced their first speaker, a Navajo Chief, who talked about the original people who had populated the area. As he neared the end of his time, he said, "The ancestors of the Navajo and Pueblo people who used to share this region, built various types of houses. The most noteworthy are the cliff dwellings."

At that point, Dr. Lightfoot interrupted. "Thank you, Chief Fire Walker." He turned his attention to the group. "Tomorrow, campers, we will visit Chaco Canyon National Historical Park to view the cliff dwellings that still exist today." Then he introduced their second speaker, a Medicine Man.

Mican knew that a Medicine Man held a position of high esteem among his people and acted as a spiritual leader, but what spirit did he lead them to? Or lead them by?

He began his presentation. "My name in the Navajo language is Ayoo ta' Be'e'sh tigaii Ooljee, it means Mighty One Silver Moon."

Ashton elbowed Mican, "Mighty One?"

He continued, "Chaco Canyon is not deep, but it is ten-miles long and located in the northwest corner of New Mexico. It is seventy miles from the nearest town, and you can get here only by rough, dirt roads. It is remote by today's standards."

Shayla leaned toward Mican. "I can vouch for the remote part. After we got off of the train at Thoreau, I thought to myself, 'this isn't so bad,' but when the jeep driver turned onto that dirt road, I thought it would never end."

Mican shushed his sister, which her now twelve-year-old-self, didn't like very much. She scrunched her lips and folded her arms.

The speaker had continued while she talked, so they missed a part, but they picked up here.

"Then the people began building in a very different manner. They constructed huge stone buildings that rose to four or five stories and contained up to seven hundred rooms and dozens of kivas."

Dr. Lightfoot stepped forward again. "Campers, a kiva is a religious structure. We will see examples of that and the cliff dwelling architecture at the park tomorrow. Sorry, Mr. Silver Moon, please continue."

"These structures were connected to one another by lines of sight that would have made fast communication possible. Often built along heavenly star and planet lines, called celestial alignments, these buildings included water-collection systems and linked outlying communities by a large network of roads with Chaco Canyon at its center. When you get home, you can Google all of this at Chaco Canyon National Historical Park's website and Wikipedia."

Chuckles floated through the group.

"Yes, I am a Native American Medicine Man, but I am *not* primitive. I *do* know how to use a computer." He laughed and smiled.

Most of the campers smiled and chuckled along with him, then he continued. "These great houses were advanced works. They were proof of an intelligent and highly skilled group of people. It is not clear why the people left Chaco Canyon, but a long water shortage is one possible reason." Silver Moon fell silent and stared intently into the campfire.

Following the pause, he scanned the campers' faces. "These missing people are sometimes called the Anasazi or the cliff dwellers. I probably should not tell you this, but another explanation for why these people are missing is that they were eaten by giants."

Snickers rumbled throughout the campers, Dr. Lightfoot stood to correct them, but the Medicine Man held up his hand to stop him.

"I know many of you today do not believe what you consider to be 'old Indian tales,' but I assure you, I have seen the bones of fallen giants. My grandfather Naana, who was also a Medicine Man, took me to a secret place where the bones are hidden. Grandfather taught me the ways of the past, and I know the giants came here through entryways from another world, portals, they are sometimes called."

Bailey smirked. "Where are these portals? Can we see one?"

Silver Moon searched the faces, his gaze landed on Bailey's smug grin. "Only Truth Seekers may find them and only the pure of heart may go through, but do not be fooled, few really want to find them. The beings on the other side are not to be treated lightly."

She met his gaze and raised one eyebrow. "You mean the giants are over there and might eat us?" She laughed and scanned the faces of the other campers. When her eyes reached Mican's, his low eyebrows stopped her cold. Her face changed and she turned back to the Medicine Man.

Dr. Lightfoot stood and glared at her. "Bailey, that will be enough out of you." He turned to his guest. "I am so sorry. Would you like to share more with us?"

Silver Moon's gaze turned to the fire again. "Only that the time for this world is short and many will be caught unaware."

Bailey folded her arms and started another eye-roll until she noticed Mican nodding in agreement with the Medicine Man.

Dr. Lightfoot turned to him. "Thank you for coming Mr. Silver Moon. It has been very informative." He glanced around the group now bathed in only flickers of firelight. "And campers, thank you for your attentiveness," but his stare rested on Bailey and he lowered his eyebrows. "You are dismissed for the evening. I will see you bright and early in the morning for our trip to Chaco Canyon National Park."

The campers stood.

Shayla grabbed Mican's shirt sleeve. "I need to talk to you. That last statement sent chills down my arms."

Bailey approached and tossed her hair. "What statement? 'You are dismissed.'" She laughed so hard, she accidentally snorted.

Her hair framed her harsh sneer, but Mican issued an invitation. "Bailey, my siblings and I usually pray before we turn in for the night. Would you like to join us?"

Her eyes opened wide and she fidgeted. "Uh, not

tonight. I have to, uh, do something." She turned and headed back to their tent.

Shayla's shoulders relaxed, she breathed out a big sigh of relief.

Ashton faced her, folded his arms and frowned.

She crossed her arms in a standoff and stepped back with one foot. "Okay Ashy, what's the matter?"

"Be nice Shay, she *just* needs to meet Abba."

Shayla leaned toward him and pointed. "Ashy, you and Bailey should get married. I've never met anyone who uses the word 'just' more than you two do." She tossed her mass of curls back and laughed.

Her brother's mouth turned down at the corners, he placed one fist on his waist and pointed at her. "You just keep your opinions to yourself, Miss Smart-mouth. No joking around like that in front of her. Savvy?"

Mican ignored their disagreement, staring off into the distance. "You are absolutely right about Bailey needing to meet Abba, Ash." He turned to his sister. "I'm sorry about pairing you with such a chatterbox, Shay, but no one else would share a tent with her. The bunk in her tent was the only girl's bed left." He smiled, but then the look in his eyes turned serious. He leaned toward them and lowered his voice. "Come with me, you two. I want to show you something."

Mican led Ashton and Shayla up a dry, dusty path to the ridge where he had stood earlier in the day and watched for their arrival.

Only a faint glow of orange lingered on the horizon; the moon illuminated the desert below. As their eyes adjusted, a spectacular view stretched out before them, the beautiful inky-black sky displayed millions of stars.

At the far edge of the plateau, Mican pointed to the desert floor below. "Look at the lines etched in the clay down there. Do you remember what the Medicine Man said about the villages being 'connected to one another by lines of sight that would have enabled rapid communication'?"

Ashton folded his arms. "Yeah, I thought that was strange. I wondered what kind of communication. Fires? Torches? Smoke signals?"

Shayla nodded at him. "Yeah, the same thought crossed my mind."

Mican pointed up the canyon. "That is where the National Park is." He adjusted his arm to point to the moonlight-bathed area at the foot of the plateau. "That line below heads straight for the heart of the park. I think it's part of the connection Silver Moon talked about and it heads straight north."

Shayla spread her hands at her sides. "How can you tell it's straight north, bubba?"

"The Medicine Man and that term creeps me out, I think I'll call him the MM."

"Sounds fine to me," said Ashton.

"Anyway, the MM said the Native Americans, often built along celestial alignments, so look for the Big Dipper."

Shayla pointed and yelled. "Found it."

"Okay, now find the Little Dipper. The North Star is at the end of its handle."

Ashton pointed. "Yep, got it."

"Can you tell that the line below, heads straight for the North Star?"

Ashton's eyes traced the marking below. "Holy Smokes. You're right."

Mican smiled and patted his brother on the back. "Thanks Ash, but can we save 'holy' for the King?"

He bobbed his head. "Sure. You're right. Sorry."

Shayla folded her arms across her body and shivered. "This is great and all, but how do we get down from here? My short sleeves worked fine for one hundred-degree temperatures, but it is getting cold out here."

Mican reached into the long pocket of his cargo shorts and pulled out a small flashlight. "This way, my lady."

Shayla laughed. "That reminds me of our visits to the King's garden. I loved it when the King said we could call him Abba. I like thinking of him as Daddy, it's so sweet and personal."

Mican shined the flashlight under his chin, casting an eerie glow onto his face. He forced his voice out deep and raspy. "You know, Shay, I have a feeling this may be another mystery-filled summer. Even though it doesn't look like the King's garden, we may find some adventure here." He laughed and shined the light onto the path. He bent his elbow and pointed it toward his sister.

Shayla hooked her arm in his and reached for Ashton. "Come on Mighty Ones, it's time to get back to camp. I can't wait to see what God has in store for us this time."

But she failed to realize how soon their mystery would begin.

Chapter 2

Petroglyphs

Shortly after sunrise, the breakfast bell clanked.

In the mess tent, Shayla ran into Mican. "Where's Ashy?"

"He has already eaten and gone back to our tent to get jackets for us. I waited here to tell you to get one for yourself."

"What? Jackets? It feels like it's already eighty degrees outside."

"I know, but Warrior told me in a dream that we would need jackets, so get one before we leave. Dr. Lightfoot said we will load the van in fifteen minutes."

Ashton appeared at the opening of the mess tent and waved to flag them toward the bus.

Shayla grabbed a breakfast burrito and a cup of orange

juice. She headed toward her tent to get a jacket, but almost ran into Bailey coming out of the shower area. She noticed Shayla's breakfast and made a gagging sound.

Mican stood nearby, his arms folded, watching his sister and laughed.

"Nice Bailey, thanks for helping me enjoy my breakfast."

"How can you eat that stuff this early in the morning? And where are you going?"

"I'm going to get a—something." Shayla fumbled for words.

"A—something. Now that's a new one. By the way, set me up with a seat on the van next to Mican or Ash-boat."

"Why do you call Ashton, Ash-boat?"

"You know, he's *just* so dreamy. Dreamboat ... Ash-boat."

Shayla groaned and rolled her eyes as she entered the tent. Seconds later, she emerged with her jacket and a fanny pack. She took the last bite of her breakfast and rushed into the girls' shower area.

The van horn honked, a young man's voice called out. "Five minutes."

She dashed toward the van, strapping on the fanny

pack as she went, pulled her shirt out over it, then tied her jacket around her waist.

Jumping onto the first step of the small bus, she looked back, her brothers were seated in the very last row. Walking down the aisle, she watched sleepy campers with tousled hair, rubbing their eyes. She took the seat in front of her brothers and watched as Bailey popped her completely made-up face and smoothed hair through the open door.

She put a little extra effort in her walk as she strolled the aisle toward the rear of the bus. "Hey, Shay-girl. Can I sit with you?"

Shayla waved at the empty seat. "Sure, help yourself."

Bailey leaned close and lowered her voice. "I thought I told you to get me a seat next to one of the babes."

"Sorry, they were already seated together when I got on."

Dr. Lightfoot stepped onto the van. "Good morning, campers. Today we will go to Chaco Canyon National Historical Park. Our time will begin with an orientation video, then our guide will take us to view the kivas and the cliff dwellings. I'm sure it is not necessary to tell you to stay with the group and to keep up. We will have a busy day."

The door of the small bus closed; Dr. Lightfoot took a seat behind the driver.

Bailey circled her index finger in the air. "Woohoo."

Her gesture stirred Mican's mischievous side, it prompted him to start a deliberately annoying conversation. "Shay, before you got on the van, I was telling Ash that I'm glad you two got to come on this tour. I have been looking forward to this since I found out I had been accepted for this project. This should be an amazing tour; don't you and Ash think so too?"

Ashton seemed well aware of what his brother was doing and joined in. "I agree totally. This is what I looked forward to the most when I found out you had gotten us permission to join the camp. Isn't that right, Shay?"

Shayla glanced at Mican and he winked, she smiled and nodded. "Uh-huh, absolutely. This should be quite a day. Don't you think so, Bailey?"

Bailey pushed a strand of hair back over her shoulder and scrunched her face. "What planet are you guys from? This is just as boring as the dirt that blows into our tents."

Mican could hardly hold back his laughter. "Speaking of what planet we're from, did you know Roswell is southeast of here? That is where they house all of the secret alien artifacts, at Area Fifty-one."

Bailey jerked her body around to face him. "If they're so secret, just how do you know about 'em?"

Shayla leaned toward Bailey. "They're not so dreamy now, are they?"

Both Mican and Ashton heard her and had to put their hands over their mouths to keep from laughing out loud.

Moments later, Bailey stood up, the bumpy road jostled her side to side. Using her hands on the back of the seats, she pulled herself along the aisle toward the front of the bus. "Dr. L., can we turn the air conditioner on? It's hot in here."

Dr. Lightfoot tried to explain. "Sorry Bailey, we can't. If we have the AC on now, then when we arrive and we're suddenly plunged into the ninety-degree heat, it could make us sick, or at the very least, we would be miserable.

Bailey walked back to her seat mumbling. "I'm already miserable, how much worse could it get?"

Not much talking happened for the next half hour, giving Shayla a much-needed break, but at times, the bumpy dirt road offered them an almost amusement-park-quality rollercoaster ride.

At last the van pulled in front of the Welcome Center and Dr. Lightfoot stood, he exited the van and a tour guide greeted him. "If you and your group will follow me, we will get you some visitor tags and start the video." The camp director stuck his head through the door, "This way, campers."

While Bailey was at the front getting her name tag, Shayla stole a minute alone with Mican and Ashton. "What's this about needing a jacket?"

Mican leaned in close. "I'm not sure. All I know is, in my dream, Warrior said for us to bring them and to stay close together."

Shayla tilted her head toward Bailey. "Okay, but did he tell you what to do about her?" and she laughed.

Bailey walked up. "What's so funny?"

Shayla struggled for an answer. "Uh, Mican told me to stay close. I guess he thinks I might get lost."

Bailey lifted her hands to the side. "That's not funny. You guys are so weird."

Ashton walked up and tapped her on the shoulder. "You know, Bailey, you are not the first person to tell us that."

He, Mican, and Shayla all laughed.

Shayla added, "Yeah, but poor Keyon, our neighbor back home, used to think we were weird, but he really loves us now."

Bailey does her trademark finger-circle. "Whoopee."

The guide began to talk so everyone tried to listen, except Bailey. She pointed behind them. "Isn't he that strange Medicine Man from last night?"

They glanced in the direction Bailey pointed. The MM stared straight at them.

Bailey looked at Mican and tipped her head toward the man. "Friend of yours?"

About that time Dr. Lightfoot called her name. "Bailey, will you join me at the front, please?"

The group started to move and the MM approached. "Good morning. I recognize you from last night." He touched Mican's elbow. "May I speak with you? Walk slowly, please."

Ashton and Shayla flanked Mican and the MM.

"My name is Ayoo ta'. I want you to know that I am a follower of the King too. Most people assume a Medicine Man cannot be a Christian, but the Spirit I follow is Abba's Spirit. An angel spoke to me last night in a dream and told me to tell you that Abba will be with you, and what you seek is on the ridge at the far end of the ruins."

Ashton interrupted. "What are you talking about? We aren't seeking anything. We are just here for summer camp."

Mican paused. "I'm afraid that's not quite true, Ash. I've known for some time now that there is something I'm supposed to do here. I wasn't quite sure what it was and I didn't know until last night that you and Shay would be part of it, but Warrior said we all needed jackets."

The Medicine Man nodded. "Ahhh, yes, Warrior, the King's stallion. I know him too. Now you must catch up to the group; tell no one we have spoken." The Medicine Man turned and walked away.

Shayla looked to her oldest brother. "Mican, I trust you, but do you have any idea what this is about?"

"No," he wiggled his fingers around over his stomach, "I've felt this stirring for quite a while, but I don't know anything specific. I'm glad Abba sent the MM to tell us he will be with us, that makes me feel a lot better. And now that I know the MM is a follower of Abba, I think we should call him something more respectful."

"His name is Mighty One Silver Moon," added Shayla. "Isn't that cool?"

Ashton pointed. "We need to step up the pace. Come on, hurry, the introductory video is starting."

***

Following the video and a bathroom break, they began their climb to the ruins. The steepness of the mountain and the heat, taxed their young muscles, but everyone made it fine with the exception of Bailey's hair and makeup.

Shayla looked at her and laughed. "Your hair looks like mine did this morning when I got up."

Bailey's hair leaned, piled up on the right side of her head with the ends sticking out every-which-way.

"Darn wind and my makeup is sliding off of my face in this heat." She sat down on a rock and wiped her face on the hem of her shirt. "So much for waterproof makeup."

Shayla shook her head. "It's still waterproof, Bay. Only you're wearing it on your shirt now, instead of on your face," and she laughed.

"You and your brothers are always laughing. I don't see anything funny."

Shayla sat next to her. "I'm sorry. Please don't be angry. This could be fun."

Dr. Lightfoot called. "Hurry up girls. We have a lot to see."

Bailey snarled. "If you've seen one kiva, you've seen 'em all."

Shayla grabbed Bailey by the elbow and pulled her to her feet.

Mican and Ashton stood close by and watched Shayla

trying to help Bailey.

Ashton pointed at the girls, but looked at his brother. "You know, she's not bad for a sister."[i]

Mican grinned and nodded. "Indeed, she's not bad at all, but stick close to her. She may need us."

Ashton walked along next to his brother. "How are we going to work this out with Bailey in the picture?"

Mican smiled and pushed his shoulders toward his ears. "I don't know, bro. That's Abba's problem."

They finally reached the cliff dwellings.

Ashton pushed his hands out to the side and turned around. "Man, this is awesome."

Shayla walked toward a sloping wall at the back. "Ashy, look at this." She glanced his direction. "Look at these petroglyphs. This wall carving looks like a family. This looks like a hunter. This must be—," and she caught her breath. "Ashy, look. Does that look like a giant to you?"

Mican walked toward them and stared at the picture. "Is it an accident that that man is drawn larger than the other figures, or is it supposed to be a giant? Hmm, Shay, I think you are right. I think it was meant to be a giant."

A voice from behind them snatched their attention. "You're all nuts. I'm now convinced." Bailey stood behind them with her hands on her hips.

Shayla tilted her head. "Bay, don't you remember what the Medicine Man said last night?"

Bailey twisted her lips. "Did you believe that load of fish bait?"

Ashton pointed at the stone wall. "Well, look."

Bailey strolled over and cut her eyes toward the wall. "Yeah, uh-huh, right."

Shayla wandered away from the group. "This looks like it used to be a window. I wonder if they had to bring all of this stuff up here from way down there?" The voice of the tour guide right behind her startled her.

"They had to carry or haul every piece of rock and clay up here and do it as they scaled the rough terrain. And think about it, they had no fast food places to pick up dinner. They had to hunt, gather, cook, and build. It was quite a large undertaking, don't you agree?"

Shayla nodded and smiled at him. "That's pretty amazing."

The tour guide flashed a broad grin at Shayla and continued his spiel. "Later, they decided to put in the path for you, city folks. Oh, by the way, that guard rail wasn't here back then either."

Ashton noticed the way the tour guide smiled at his sister, he pursed his lips and stepped closer.

Mican chuckled, but after all, he had told Ashton to stick close to her, so he didn't tease him.

While the guide posed for pictures with various members of the group, Shayla reminded her brothers of what Silver Moon had said. "What we seek is on the ridge at the far end of the ruins. I wonder if these are the ruins he meant?" She pointed out past where the guide had taken them. "And I wonder if that is the 'far end'?"

Mican took his hands from his pockets and scratched his head. "Well, I guess we need to go have a look, don't you think?"

Chapter 3

What You Seek

They moseyed away from the group and wandered toward the far tip of the ridge. Mican led the way, but when he had gone as far as he could go, he looked at his brother and sister, then shrugged his shoulders. "Nada. I got 'nuthin.'"

Shayla placed her hands on the wall and looked south into the distance. "Look at that." She pointed. "Could that be the other end of the line we saw from the ridge last night?"

Ashton leaned over and followed the line in the sand all the way to the base of the plateau where they stood. "That has to mean something. We are standing in a direct line with camp and where the North Star was last night."

Mican scratched his chin. "But what does it mean? Come on, we need to head back to the group." Mican passed Shayla who still stared into the distance.

Ashton stepped past her too, clearing a line of sight to an archway in the outer wall. In the middle of the arch, a dust devil began to form. Shayla turned to face her brothers, but at the same time she pointed toward the strange sight. "Boys, look."

Ashton turned and watched Shayla's outstretched arm pass into the whirlwind. At that moment, the swirling funnel of air began to pull her off balance and suck her into the opening. Ashton lunged toward her, grabbed her arm, and yelled, "Shay," right before her head passed through the window.

The whirling vortex now threatened to devour Ashton; his arm and shoulder disappeared.

Mican launched himself toward his brother and grabbed his ankle with both hands, but the force of the vortex pulled Ashton through, before sucking Mican into its grip.

Dizzy and floaty Mican spun in the whirlwind. He tried to yell. "Shay, are you okay?" but his words became slurred, like they were stretched out, pulled thin by the air. Strange questions raced through his mind. Is this a time warp? Or a wormhole? No, it must be a portal like Silver

Moon talked about. He heard a *plunk*, Shayla must have landed on the ground. Another *plunk*, Ashton must have landed too, then a *plop*, he landed on his stomach next to them. It took a few seconds for him to catch his breath, then he asked, "Are y'all okay?"

"I think so," said Shayla.

"Yeah, me too," said Ashton. "What about you, bro?"

"I got the wind knocked out of me, but I think I'm in one piece. Did we fall off of the cliff or something?

Shayla stood and tried to put it into words. "I saw a dust devil, then I accidentally put my hand too close when I was pointing at it; the next thing I knew, I was skimming across some clouds, then *ker-plunk*. I landed here."

Ashton pulled his knees to his chest and brushed his pants legs. "Yep, that pretty much describes it, except, where is here?"

"I don't know, but let me see if I can get up." Mican groaned as he tried to stand.

They each shook their arms, stretched their backs and rotated their necks.

Ashton sighed. "Man, I do feel like I've been thrown off of a cliff."

"Me too," said Shayla. "I think I may have a bruise on my backside, but poor Mican, I think I heard your bones rattle when you hit."

As he stretched to his full height, he smiled at her. "Is that a reference to how skinny I am, Shay?"

Ashton walked forward a couple of steps. "Guys, I think you will want to see this."

His brother and sister stepped toward him.

Mican glanced over a wall. "Oh brother," then he turned to look behind them.

Still confused, Shayla asked, "Where are we?"

Ashton turned to look at her, "I don't think that's the right question. We are right back where we started from. The question is, when are we here?"

They stood on a high ridge. A partial wall of rocks stood nearby, but no guardrail existed.

Shayla backed up. "Oh, boy. What do we do now?"

Mican wrapped his fingers around her arm and lowered his voice. "Hide."

From the other end of the ridge, voices drifted toward them. Mican pulled his sister. "Come with me, behind this rock."

Ashton scrambled over it and plonked in next to them. They heard men talking, but couldn't understand what they said.

Mican leaned between his brother and sister, keeping

his voice low. "They must be Anasazi."

Shayla spoke equally low. "Maybe they can help us."

Ashton squinted at her. "Maybe they might throw us off of their mountain for trespassing."

Chapter 4

Bones of the Giants

A deep, smooth voice filled the air. "Come out. I know you are here. You are safe."

Mican paused for a moment and put his finger to his lips. He eased his head up above the top of the boulder that concealed them. "Who are you?"

Mican faced a Native American man, probably only a little older than himself. His angular face and long jet-black hair shone in the sunlight.

"I am Naana Silver Moon. Naana, in your language means, Another Time. This is my brother Oot'l which means Vision. We have been expecting you. Abba told us you are Truth Seekers and that you would come. We are here to help you."

Mican's eyebrows jumped up. "Abba? You know the King?"

"Yes, our names together mean we are your Vision from Another Time. Abba told our parents before our births what we should be named. We have known him for many years. He told us when and where to expect you. The King said you *and* your brother and sister would be here today."

Ashton and Shayla rose from where they were crouched.

Naana smiled at them. "Hello."

Shayla replied. "Hello. Do you know Ayoo ta'?"

Naana tilted his head back. "Ayoo ta'? Is that to be his name? Mighty One. My son has not yet been born, but I look forward to meeting him—and my grandson Ayoo ta' in the future."

Ashton looked at Mican and shouted, probably a little louder than he intended. "We were with Ayoo ta' this morning, now we have arrived before his father's birth. That's awesome."

Naana's white teeth stood out against the dark tan of his face. "You must be the Mighty One called Ashton."

Ashton's eyebrows wrinkled and his hands shot out to his sides. "How does everybody know who I am?"

Shayla and Mican looked at each other and laughed.

Naana grinned and continued. "Abba's Spirit guided

me here to meet you. Here are some food packages and three blankets."

"Blankets?" shouted Shayla. "How long are we going to be here?"

"Until you have completed your quest for truth," replied Naana.

"What quest for truth?" asked Ashton. "I didn't ask for anything. Did you, Mican?"

"Hmmm. Yeah, this could be my fault."

Shayla shrank back. "What did you do?"

"You see, when Ayoo ta' talked about what his grandfather had told him about the Anasazi being eaten by giants, I remembered the verse in Genesis about the giants, so I started studying last night and I wondered what it meant."

"How did that get us here?" asked Ashton.

Naana answered. "Yes, my grandfather's grandfather told us of the giants. The people of this place where you stand were laid waste overnight by an attack of the giants. Grandfather said a few people escaped to nearby villages, but most were eaten. Many of the neighboring settlers survived because they were warned and found safety in the forests and in caves. Some decided to blame drought or lack of rain for the missing Anasazi, but others like my grandfather's ancestors, passed down the truth.

Ashton scratched his chin. "Okay, so how does that get us here—now? This must be at least a hundred years in our past."

The handsome young Native American continued. "Abba told me to meet you here, give you food and blankets and guide you to another travel circle. We must go. Come. We must hurry."

"Go where?" asked Mican.

Naana leaned close to him. "Abba wants me to show you the bones of the giants."

Shayla's mouth flew open and her shoulders bounced toward her ears. "Really! We actually get to see them? That's scary and exciting."

"No need to be afraid, Mighty One Shayla. Abba's Spirit is with us and wants you to understand."

"Okay." Mican headed toward the ladder where Naana and his brother had climbed onto the ledge, but Oot'l corrected his direction by touching his elbow and pointing to the other side of the cliff. Directly opposite the ladder Naana and Oot'l climbed up, another portal lay hidden. Naana extended his arm. "Abba says to go this way."

They followed him, as he walked straight into a

swirling vortex. Oot'l motioned for them to hold hands and step in behind his brother. Mican took Shayla's hand before stepping in, she reached back for Ashton as Mican disappeared. They quickly swirled and bumped. At the other end, Mican landed on his feet.

Shayla rushed in behind him, he reached to help her stay on her feet, but she needed no help, she also arrived upright. "Wow, I feel dizzy, but at least I'm standing this time." She laughed. "My tush is still sore from that first time."

At that moment, Ashton came through as if seated on a horse. He didn't quite get his feet under his body, before the swirl disappeared. He plopped down, deposited onto his bottom, his knees bent in front of him. "Ow!"

Mican stuck out a hand to help him up. Ashton stood rubbing his backside. Looking around he realized they were in a different place. "Where are we, Naana?"

"We are on the far side of the plateau, at the desert floor. Come this way, we will have to crawl to enter this cave. The entrance has been blocked to prevent strangers from finding it." He dropped to his knees, then his stomach and crawled toward a shadow.

Ashton looked at Mican and gestured toward the rock wall. "Be my guest, dude."

Mican shook his head. "Thanks, bro. I really appreciate you allowing me to take the lead."

Ashton laughed. "No prob, bro."

He knelt on the hot, dry sand and stretched out, his body became uncomfortably warm. Using the part of his arms between his elbows and wrists, Mican dragged himself under the edge of the rock. Entering the darkness, the ground beneath him felt cooler. The deeper under the plateau he crawled, the cooler the sand and air became.

With a tremor in her voice, his sister asked, "Bubba, will you tell us what it's like?"

"Don't worry, Shay-belle. Remember, Abba is in control."

"I know, but it would still be nice to know what we are getting ourselves into."

Ashton patted her on the shoulder. "Do you want me to go next? I'm sure Oot'l will crawl in after you."

"No, Ashy, I will go next, if that's okay with you."

Ashton waved his hand. "Be my guest, sis."

Each made their way through the small opening. Once inside, they stood in pitch black darkness with their backs against the wall.

Naana must have struck his knife against a piece of

flint, a spark produced a small flicker, then all of a sudden, a nearby torch crackled into a flame. When it grew, it revealed the expanse of a towering cavern. Their eyes quickly adjusted to the torchlight and to the massive space. Stuffy, dry air filled their nostrils. He lit another torch and passed it to his brother, as it swept past in front of them, it smelled like a wax candle burning, but much stronger.

They held the torches high over his head. "This was the assembly hall of the giants. The passages to your left and right," he gestured in each direction, "lead to a network of living areas. If you will follow me through here," he pointed straight ahead, "this is the ancient burial chamber."

Shayla reached for Mican's arm. "Can I hold onto you, just in case?"

"In case of what, Shay?"

"I don't know…that's why it's 'just in case.'"

Ashton chuckled. "They are dead, Shay. Bones you know, not giants."

Naana led them through a doorway.

When the torchlight filled the room, even Ashton gasped. "I…I can't believe how…."

Mican placed his hand on Shayla's hand that gripped

his arm. "You okay, Shay-belle?"

Shayla gulped audibly, her voice sounded so tiny in the great space. "I'm all right, bubba, but I'm glad I'm holding your arm. I feel like I'm being sucked toward the middle of the room."

"You are correct, Mighty One Shayla. There is a powerful travel circle in the center of this space. The bones have been placed around the sides of the chamber to enhance the power of the portal. This is one of the places where the giants entered our world."

Ashton walked toward some bones, when he stood beside them, he realized they were a complete skeleton lying next to the wall. "Mican, look at this."

Still holding Shayla's hand, Mican pulled her along with him.

She shivered as they approached. "Wow, Ashy, this guy must be over ten feet tall."

Ashton pointed at Mican. "Bro, you are just about six feet tall. Lie down next to him."

Mican chuckled. "Ash, do you want to use me as a measuring stick?"

"Well, maybe I do." He grinned at his lanky brother.

Shayla turned loose of his arm. "Go ahead, bubba. Give it a try." As she took a step back, her arms swung out to the sides and her feet skidded on the sandy floor.

Her brothers lunged and grabbed her arms.

Ashton breathed out a sigh. "Gee-wiz, Shay! Where did you think you were going?"

"It felt like I was made of metal and a magnet had a hold of me, pulling me to the middle of the room."

"Okay, Ash, if I'm going to do this, you are going to have to be an anchor for Shay."

Ashton covered one eye and growled. "Yo ho, matey, if it's an anchor you're after, I'll hold 'er down."

Shayla pulled her arm away from him. "Very funny, Ash-tray."

Her brothers tossed their heads back and laughed.

Ashton continued with his pirate's growl. "Aye, she's a feisty 'un, capt'n."

She resisted their attention until she began to skid backwards again, against her will; she flung her arms out and Ashton grabbed her, pulling his sister toward him. "Okay, bubba I'll hold on to you. Sorry I was being so feisty." She clung to his arm and smiled.

Mican squatted on the sandy slab of stone, placed his hands behind his bottom and sat down. Stretching his legs out, he adjusted himself so the soles of his shoes lined up with the giant's feet and he stretched out flat. "Okay, Ash, check this out. Are my feet even with his?"

Ashton checked the feet then stepped toward Mican's head. His jaw dropped. "Dude, the top of your head is up to where his waist would be." He marked the sand with the toe of his blue sneaker. "Slide your feet up to here."

Mican lifted his bottom and crab-walked to Ashton's line.

Ashton checked the line, as Mican stretched out. "Okay, how's this?"

Shayla gasped. "What!"

Ashton rubbed his chin with his free hand. "Man! This guy was over twelve-feet tall!"

Mican rotated his head to the side and saw the bottom jaw of the gigantic skull. "No way! He was more than twice as tall as me. That's amazing!" At that moment, Mican heard a *rattle.* "Naana, are there snakes in here?"

"Yes, Mighty One, and they only warn once, slide yourself away from the bones; no sudden moves and you should be all right."

As Mican slid his body away from the skeleton, Shayla repeated, "Should be alright. We need to get out of here."

Mican worked himself away from the skeleton and stood. "Naana, how many giants were there?

He slowly panned his torch around the room, piles of bones lay against the wall in every direction.

Ashton shouted. "Whoa! There must be dozens of 'em."

"You are correct, Mighty One Ashton. That skeleton was left complete. He must have been an important figure, but the other areas are stacked high with leg bones, arm bone, and other bits, heaved against the walls." He flashed his torch to the far side. "The pile of skulls bothers me the most, the eyes are particularly disturbing. No one has dared to count them to learn the exact number."

Ashton turned to walk to the center of the room, the magnetic pull locked onto his limbs. His arms flew out into a zombie like pose, pointing to the center of the cavern. "This is so creepy and cool at the same time." He cast a glance at Naana. "Do we go to the center of the floor now, to time-warp out of here?"

"No, no! Please, step back. You do not want to go to where these giants came from. We will leave the way we came in. Follow me."

They followed Naana back to the first chamber, then crawled outside.

Shayla pointed to the stone archway. "Travel circle? Is that what that is? Another one pulled us through and dumped us here in your time."

"Yes," replied Naana. "It has many names and one can never tell where he, or she will find themselves, many of our people who left, never returned."

The arch quickly whisked them away.

"Oh boy!" said Shayla.

Chapter 5

Travel Plans

Mican, Shayla, and Ashton arrived at their starting point, gathered their provisions, then followed Naana and his brother down the steep embankment to the desert floor.

At the foot of the plateau, Shayla pointed. "Look, that's where the Visitor Center will be built in sixty years or so. Can you believe this?"

"This is a new one, even for us," said Ashton and turned to his brother. "Thanks, bro."

Mican grinned and laid his hand on his brother's shoulder. "My pleasure, I was only thinking about your education, Ash."

A blaze of orangey-red faded into the horizon as they trekked south, away from the cliff dwellings. The moon crept up lazily, then shone brightly and lit their path.

Mican glanced at Oot'l who only smiled. "Naana, why doesn't Oot'l ever speak to us?"

"Abba gave me your language so I could guide you on your journey, but he did not give it to my brother. He does not speak your words, but agreed to accompany me."

"That was nice of him, please tell him we are thankful."

Naana turned to his brother and interpreted, then said, "Oot'l wishes for you to know, you are most welcome."

Hours ticked by before they came to a stop. "We must climb up onto that table-mountain." Naana pointed up a steep cliff.

"Oh great," sighed Shayla. "Just what my legs want."

"Mighty One Shayla, we will wait here for sunrise, then we will climb. It is too dangerous at night. Come, get some rest."

"Mican, dude, this must be the backside of the plateau where the archeological camp will be located—in a hundred years or so." Ashton laughed.

"I think you are right, Ash. We must be at the west end of that plateau."

Naana smiled. "You are correct Mighty Ones, now rest."

They unrolled their blankets and tried to sleep. The

long walk had worn them out, so the hard ground wasn't much of a challenge.

***

The hot rays of the sun painted Mican's face, he sat up slowly. Close by, Naana cooked over a fire.

"Good morning, Mighty One. I hope you slept well."

"Good morning, Naana. Thank you, I slept fine."

At that point, Ashton and Shayla stirred, their brother couldn't resist teasing them. "Good morning, sleepy heads."

Naana called to them. "You must rise and eat. We need to climb on the shaded side of the table-mountain before the sun reaches its peak in the sky."

Mican looked around. "Where's Oot'l?"

"He has gone ahead of us to find water and to scout a safe route." Naana had removed the thorns and hairy spikes from some large, flat cactus leaves and roasted them on sticks over the fire. "Here. Eat something. We must move soon."

Naana's brother returned with five skin pouches full of water. Shayla thanked him, then proceeded to drink, allowing water to drip down her chin.

"Careful Mighty One. Water will be the most prized possession you have on your journey."

"I'm sorry." She cautiously tied the water bag closed and attached it to her belt loop.

The sun had fully risen on the Eastern horizon by the time they finished their meal. Naana smothered the fire with dirt and they began to climb, this time Oot'l led the way.

They paid close attention as they followed him up the steep side of the table-rock. The sun warmed the air; every inch they climbed, every inch closer to the top of the plateau, the temperature rose a degree. Zigzagging up the face of the cliff required strength and energy, they stopped every hour to sip from their water bags and to rest for a moment.

On one of those stops, Mican asked a question. "Naana, are you a medicine man?"

"I am in training to be an MM," and he chuckled.

Mican smiled. "How does it work being a Medicine Man if you are a follower of Abba?"

"My grandfather, who is a Medicine Man is teaching me. Let's say a person comes to him complaining of weakness, fatigue and sadness, Grandfather would tell them to walk out to Snake Mountain, about a half mile from the village. On his way, he is to pick up three stones and name each one. One would be named fatigue, one weakness and one sadness. When he reaches Snake Mountain, he is to throw the stones, one at a time, as far as he can throw them, telling each to flee from his body and not return. He is to do this every morning for a month, rain or shine. At the end of the month he is to come back to see my grandfather."

Shayla's eyebrows sat low over her eyes. "Do spirits enter into the rocks and then he throws them away?"

Naana laughed hardily. "No, the villager has walked a mile each day getting exercise and has bent over at least three times, stretching his back and has exercised his throwing arm three times a day for a month. He is in much better health and more physically fit, so he feels better. At the end of the month when the patient returns to grandfather, he would tell him or her to continue the activity three times a week for the rest of his life."

Ashton laughed and shouted. "That's brilliant!"

"That's Abba," said Naana. "For some ailments there are plants and herbs, but no mumbo-jumbo, as you might say."

"That is fabulous," said Mican. "I hope we didn't offend you."

Naana laughed good naturedly. "No, your ignorance was quite entertaining."

Mican burst out laughing.

***

Several hours after breaking camp, they reached the flat top of the plateau. As they each rose above the rim, the sun hit them full in the face. Naana moved across the semi-smooth plateau to an area with a small outcropping of rocks. "Sit here in the shadow."

"What now?" asked Ashton.

"As the shadow shrinks, we will know it is time."

In his usual manner, Ashton lifted his shoulders and spread his hands. "Time for what?"

Before Naana could answer, Mican pointed to a large stone with an archway, standing at the end of their sheltered area. "Are we going to jump through there?"

Naana smiled. "Yes, Mighty One. The next leg of your journey will begin when the sun is fully overhead in the sky and when this shadow vanishes, so will you."

"Oh great." shouted Ashton, as his arms flapped out to the side and down again.

Shayla stared at him. "Where will we go?"

"I do not know, Mighty One Shayla. My job ends here at the height of the sun, but Abba's Spirit will be your guide. You need to eat from your stores and drink before your journey begins; remember to fill your pouches every time there is water. Now rest before the sun finds you."

The shadow of the rock, shaded their faces, they ate a bite and sipped some water.

Shayla's pouch was almost dry, she glanced at Mican, but Naana noticed her distress. "Do not worry, Mighty One, Abba knows your every need. Rest now."

A few minutes more, as the sun peeked over their shelter, their shade receded. "Arise Mighty Ones, come with me."

They stood and followed their guide to the edge of the plateau.

Naana looked back. Only a tiny sliver of shade remained. "When the sun reaches its height, the shade will totally disappear and you will enter the portal. Mican, you must go first. Step through as you would through any doorway and the landing will be less rough. You will hold Shayla's hand and she will follow you. Mighty One Ashton, you will hold your sister's other hand and be pulled through behind her. Stay upright and you will land on your feet."

Mican turned and grabbed Naana's hand and wrist. "I want to thank you and Oot'l for following Abba and for all you have done to help us."

Naana glanced back at the rock.

Their eyes followed his gaze. They saw the sun creep over the top of their shelter and the shade below vanished. He yelled, "Go now."

Mican loosed his grip on Naana, grabbed Shayla's hand and stepped into the arch, his right foot disappeared.

Naana and Oot'l began to sing praises to Abba and his Son.

Ashton grabbed Shayla's other arm. Mican zipped away, pulling Shayla behind him, Ashton stepped forward and instantly joined his siblings, leaving their new friends alone on the plateau.

***

Skimming across clouds. Lightly bouncing. Shadows. Brightness. Darkness. Spinning. Lying flat. Sitting on air. The time seemed endless as they traveled to who-knew-where.

Mican tried to speak, but his words were again thinned by the air. His body experienced weightlessness, then heaviness. Fear gripped him, until a familiar voice reassured him. "Fear not, I am with you." Instantly, he jolted as he landed.

Shayla bounced in behind him and Ashton followed.

Mican asked, "Is everyone okay?"

Ashton shouted. "Whoa. What a ride. It was different

this time."

Mican pulled Shayla in close to him, which pulled Ashton too, because they still firmly held her wrists.

"I think I'm okay. Are you and Ashy all right?"

Mican laughed, but studied the area. "I'm fine Shay. Much better landing this time."

Shayla now understood why he had pulled her close. They stood on the edge of a stream that looked very much like the piranha-stream in the garden.[ii] She drew back, pulling Ashton with her.

Mican took the lead, loosening his grip on her, he knelt next to the shallow creek. "Let's fill our water bags while we can. I don't see any fish, but hurry."

Ashton realized he still held tightly to Shayla and laughed.

They all bent quietly by the stream and refilled their pouches. Each of them took a big drink and topped off the oiled leather skins, then secured the bags of treasured water to their belt loops. They stood again and looked around.

"At least we seem to be on Abba's side of the creek this time," said Ashton.

"Yes," said Mican, "but we are not sure this is the same stream. We need to stay on guard."

Mican remembered the whisper in his ear. "I heard the Spirit when we were in the portal, he told me not to be afraid. Did either of you hear him?"

"I heard him say 'prepare for the landing,'" said Ashton. "I was told to bend my knees slightly and to hold on to you, Shay."

"I heard nada," said Shayla with a slight scowl.

Mican gestured to his siblings. "Come on, we need to pray." They stepped away from the stream and joined hands. "Ash, you lead off."

"Abba, we are here—wherever here is. We thank you for this journey. We want to be obedient and we want to find the truth you sent us to seek. Guide us, please. In the name of your Son. Amen."

They opened their eyes and there in the trees, Ashton saw a faint outline of the dove and pointed. "There, look. There's the Spirit."

They each saw the Spirit and turned to follow him as he led the way and soon they entered a familiar-looking area.

"What is this? Where are we?" asked Ashton. "Are we back in the garden? Are we back home?"

The dove fluttered in close to the Mighty Ones. "You are in the garden, but you are not back home. In fact, your home does not exist yet, nor do you."

"How can that be?" asked Shayla.

Mican answered. "Remember what Abba told us about time? He knows all of time. We have journeyed into the past."

"But how far 'into the past,'" asked Shayla.

"I guess we will have to wait to find out, it's probably more of our training," said Ashton with a smile.

"Very true Mighty One, now follow me closely." The dove led them up a path to the cliff that Shayla once feared.

She pointed. "Look, a place to rest has been carved out of the hillside since our last visit," she paused and cocked her head, "or was it filled in before our first visit? This is all a little confusing."

The Spirit instructed them. "Sit here, rest and eat a bite of your food, while I gather more supplies for you."

They sat with their backs to the all-too-familiar cliff.

Ashton surprised them when he shared. "I have always assumed this was the backside of the dragon's den because I can hear water running out from over there," and he pointed toward the far curve of the mountain. "But now I realize that can't be true because we are on Abba's side of the stream. The dragon's cave can't be here."[iii]

Peace washed over them as they sat enjoying the scenery. Abba Father's castle stood majestically in the distance, surrounded by the familiar stone wall, the river sparkled as it flowed from under the far side and down the rolling hill, into the lake. All *seemed* as it had on their last visit.

When the dove returned, he carried a large leaf, which had been gathered up at the points. It was brimming full with fruits, nuts and berries. The leaf-packet resembled the small sacks of food they had received from Naana. The dove placed the package on the ledge. "Replenish your food supplies quickly, you will rest here until you witness what you have been brought here to see, then I will guide you to the next travel portal and send you on your way."

"You mean we don't get to visit Abba?" shouted Shayla.

"Not this time Mighty One. There is much trouble stirring in the Kingdom tonight. Rest now, I will awaken you when it is time."

Chapter 6

The Rebellion

It was night when the dove woke them, the moon shone palely, only a few stars speckled the sky. The castle they had only known in the bright of day, appeared so different in the dark, but as their eyes became accustomed to the dim light, they discerned thousands of dark figures filling the air over the fortress.

They sat up straight and fixed their eyes on the castle. Mican, Ashton, and Shayla's vision narrowed as the Spirit focused their eyes into the palace. A brilliant, shining green creature strutted before the throne.

Shayla pointed and yelled. "That is how the dragon looked to me when I was under his spell."

Abba's voice boomed as they had never heard it before. "You have betrayed me. You tried to exalt yourself above me, Morning Star."

The luminous being tilted his chin and responded. "I am beautiful. I fill your kingdom with music and song. I deserve the praise of your followers."

Abba's voice thundered in reply. "I cannot allow this behavior. You and your foolish followers are cast out of my Kingdom. You will never live here again. Be gone."

Without warning, a sound like the crack of a whip *snapped,* then thunder *rumbled* over the kingdom. They witnessed the beautiful, shining, green figure lifted high above the castle. Then, a streak of lightning broke through the sky as Abba threw the evil worship leader head-long to the ground. The earth shook beneath their feet.[iv]

With terrible anger, the throng of creatures screeched, screamed and howled, as the ugly band of fallen ones swirled above the castle, yet they never dared to swoop low. In a frenzy, the dark swarm whipped themselves into a tornado-like fit, but with another flash of light, they too were cast out.

The sky became calm and light began to cover the castle once again, but the dove sadly spoke. "How art thou fallen from heaven, O Lucifer, son of the morning. How art thou cut down to the ground, which didst weaken the nations!"[v]

The Mighty Ones stood, speechless.

Finally, Mican spoke. "This is the rebellion Warrior told us about. We have witnessed the dragon—the worship leader and his followers being cast out of the Kingdom."

Suddenly a window opened before them, a movie screen came into view. A beautiful lush garden, lay before them. A light breeze swayed the leaves and grass. Warm, gentle sunlight filled the area, but the scene changed. They could see the head of a beautiful woman who strolled behind a bush, her long hair draped over her shoulders, but then a snake-like serpent slithered up to her and started talking.

Shayla blurted out. "His voice sounds like the dragon's."

Then the woman reached for a piece of fruit from a tree.

Shayla yelled a warning. "No. Don't eat it," but the woman took a big bite.

The scene changed again, a man joined the woman in the picture, he took a piece of fruit from her hand.

Shayla leaned forward to yell again, but Mican grabbed her by the arm. "It's no use, Shay. They can't hear you."

Ashton sighed. "We just witnessed the fall of

mankind."

They were snapped back to the moment by the voice of the dove. "Quickly now. We must get you to safety before the dragon and his followers find you in the garden."

Mican yelled. "What?"

The dove repeated. "Come quickly."

They followed him obediently, retracing their steps down the path they had used to climb to the cliff. When they arrived at the stream, the dove directed them. "Cross here. I will dry your clothes when you reach the other side."

"But you can't come with us if we cross over," said Shayla.

"You will be fine." He pointed with his wing, "Walk quickly, in a straight line and you will arrive at your next travel portal. Enter the archway as soon as you arrive. Do not look back. Go now."

Mican fixed his fingers around Shayla's arm and they wildly splashed through the stream, Ashton followed close on their heels. As promised, their clothes instantly dried when they stepped out of the water.

The forest blurred as Mican ran in a straight line, or as

straight as he could manage, racing through the trees. Shayla and Ashton stayed close behind.

Very soon, looming before them, stood an opening that looked more like a doorway than an arch, but without hesitation Mican seized Shayla by the wrist and stepped forward. Shayla threw her hand back to grab Ashton, he took hold without question and the portal pulled them through.

This time, they rose and their bodies remained upright. They passed through darkness, coldness, then pale light. Mican called out, "Bend your knees," right before they dropped to the ground.

It took a moment for the dizziness to clear from their heads, then Ashton asked, "Where do you think we are this time?"

In the distance, some huts of stone lay at the bottom of the hill. As they walked forward, Ashton froze.

"Hold up, guys. We need to wait here."

Being used to Ashton receiving instructions from the Spirit, Mican and Shayla immediately stopped, but Mican asked, "What's up Ash?"

"I don't know, but I heard to 'stay here' and 'watch,' so let's get comfy and eat a snack."

"Right," chuckled Mican. "You would follow that

command by eating a snack."

They all laughed lightly and took shelter under a strange-looking tree on the hillside near where they landed. Its trunk was twisted, the branches spread out for good shade, amongst the slender leaves were nestled dots of green and black. "What are these?" asked Ashton as he looked up.

Mican reached up touching one. "They look like olives, but I've never seen them on the tree before, only in jars."

After biting into one of the fresh olives, Ashton spat it out. "The green ones are bitter. What do they do to them when they put them in jars? They don't taste like that."

About to pop one into her mouth, Shayla changed her mind. "Thanks, Ashy, I'll try a black one." She tossed the dark morsel into her mouth. "Hmmm, not my first choice of food, but it's edible."

They sat and watched the houses below. Young women came out to draw water from a well at the center of the village. Large heavy pitchers rested on their shoulders, they lowered them and attached lengths of rope. Each vessel, in turn was lowered, then hauled back, dripping wet and set upon the wall surrounding the well.

"Poor things, all that hard work. No indoor

plumbing," said Shayla, then she decided to lie back. While she reclined on the sandy soil beneath the tree, Shayla looked up through the leaves and whispered, "Boys, look. Up there."

Chapter 7

Fallen Ones

Mican and Ashton scooted over next to her and peered upward. Through the branches they saw a huge gray cloud hovering above the ridge of the hillside. Large, gross-looking figures leaned over the edge and stared into the valley below.

Their voices filtered down through the leaves of the tree.

"They are lovely and fair. We should claim them for our wives."[vi]

"You know it is forbidden. We will be punished."

"Maybe so, but if we do this, we will leave our mark upon the men of earth."

Without warning the two vile creatures swooped down into the village below and each snatched a young woman. The evil pair whisked the girls away, kicking and screaming.

Shayla sat bolt upright. "We have to do something. Mican, please."

Mican thought for a moment. "Shayla, what can we do? It's like when the dragon scooped up Ash. All we could do was pray."

Shayla began praying. "Abba, please help us. Please rescue those girls."

The dove appeared. "Mighty One, this is all in the past. You are simply watching what has already happened. The harm has already been done. These are some of the dragon's followers. This scene was played out far in the past all over the populated world."

She cried to her brothers. "It's too late. It's already done."

The sky seemed to open, she and her brothers watched scene-after-scene where women were kidnapped by hideous creatures. Streak-after-streak of darkness and light, revealed the passage of time. The Mighty Ones watched as the women eventually returned to their villages, but with them they brought the offspring of the fallen ones.[vii]

Again, the sky darkened and lightened, one time after another. The Mighty Ones saw the hybrid children, each being half-human, half-fallen creature, as they grew large and of great strength. The people surrounding them considered these giants to be heroes. They were even given a special name, the Nephilim.[viii]

"I don't like it here," whined Shayla. "I want to go home."

Mican put his arm around Shayla's shoulder. "Come on Shay. Toughen up. It's over now. It's all in the past, remember?"

Then Mican heard in his spirit, "Is it, my son? Is it over? Is it all in the past?"

Mican was confused. What did that mean? But the only answer he received was, "Rest here tonight."

They settled under the olive tree, it didn't take long to be lulled to sleep by the sound of a light breeze in the leaves above them. The next morning, they awoke to the sound of the villagers below. Mican, Ashton, and Shayla took a few minutes to eat a bite and to drink some water from their pouches which were almost empty.

The outline of the dove appeared again. "Gather your things, stay low and follow me." He led them over the crest of the hill and down the other side. "Go now to the travel arch at the bottom of this hill. When you reach it, join hands and Mican will step through first. As soon as you arrive at your new location, go to the top of the highest hill and find shelter. Stay there until you learn all you need to know."

"Will we find water there?" asked Shayla. "Our pouches are almost empty and I'm thirsty."

Chapter 8

Water

They gathered their blankets and supplies, Mican bent low and led the way, following behind the dove. When they passed the crest of the hill the dove vanished. Mican continued toward the portal with Shayla and Ashton close behind. The stony slope made walking difficult. As soon as he knew they had reached a safe distance, Mican stood tall and stretched. His siblings copied his example.

They slipped and slid on the stony, sandy hill, but in less than an hour, they reached the travel site. "Is everyone ready?" asked Mican.

He extends his left hand toward Shayla and she clasped on, then she reaches for Ashton, who loosely took hold of her wrist. "Come on, Ashy. Hold on tighter."

"I'm quite okay, thank you," Ashton replied.

Mican stepped into the archway which jerked him in quickly, Ashton felt the jolt and tightened his grip. Spinning and whirling, they bumped across soft, feathery clouds, but the landing was not quite so pleasant. They plunked out on the other end, atop a large, flat rock.

Ashton landed, way too close to the edge for comfort and scurried toward Shayla.

Mican landed on his feet, but hit abruptly, his face squeezed tight in pain, "Owww. My ankle."

"Are you okay, bubba?"

Mican examined his foot and ankle, which had already begun to swell. "I forgot to bend my knees and jammed my foot down too hard on the rock. Wow-wee this, hurts."

Ashton recalled what the Spirit had told them and looked around. "We need to go to the top of that hill and find shelter."

With Shayla's help, Mican pulled himself up and stood on one foot. "I'm going to need your help, Ash."

"Come 'ere, Gimpy," said Ashton with a playful grin. "Come to your little brother." Ashton stepped close, placed Mican's over his shoulders, then Ashton slid his arm around Mican's back. He placed his shoulder in Mican's armpit and scrunched up his face. "If you could try not to sweat, it would be greatly appreciated."

Mican laughed. "I will be sure to try, just for you, little brother."

Shayla carried all three blankets to make the walk easier.

The mountain, littered with small, loose stones and several larger ones, made travel slow and dangerous. Mican slipped and fell, nearly pulling Ashton down with him. Behind them, Shayla dropped the blankets to catch him. He almost knocked her over like a bowling pin.

"Wooo, thanks Shay-belle, I would have hated to slide all the way back to the bottom and have to start over. You would think that having Ashton's shoulder in my armpit would be comfortable, but … it's not!" He chuckled.

It took a lot of time to reach the summit, very tired and thirsty, they finally arrived. Mican and Ashton emptied their water pouches, only Shayla had any water left, she took a sip and offered to share, but Mican refused. "No Shay, you keep it. You may need it later."

"But Mican," she whined, "you need to drink some more water."

Ashton said, "Don't worry, Shay, Abba will provide."

Shayla placed her hands on her hips. "Then why won't you drink some of my water if you are so sure?"

Ashton looked at Mican and sheepishly took her

pouch. After taking a sip, he passed it to Mican who also took a drink. "Do you feel better now, Mighty One?" asked Mican with a smile.

"Yes, as a matter of fact, I do," she puffed out her cheeks. "Now we need to find some shelter."

Ashton surveyed the mountain and spotted an overhang of rocks that would provide a little shade and protection. "Look up there, that might be a good place to get out of the sun for a while."

With some effort, they helped Mican to the shady overhang, he sat down. Ashton stood next to him and tiptoed. On a plain below, Ashton caught sight of something. "I don't believe it. Guys, look at this."

Shayla stood on a big rock next to Ashton, but Mican stayed seated. "What is it, Ash?"

Shayla answered. "I really think you are going to want to see this." She jumped down to help Mican stand on his good foot and lean on her. When he finally balanced, he looked toward the plain.

Mican gasped. "No way. Can this be true?" There, in the distance on the rugged plain, stood a large, wooden boat. "Can that be Noah's ark?"

Shayla pointed. "Look." Two cheetahs approached the side of the gigantic structure, the open door acted as a ramp, the sleek animals easily climb inside. Two chimpanzees followed, along with some other animals too small to identify from this far away. There they stood and watched for a long time as two-by-two, a long procession of creatures walked into the belly of the boat.

Mican finally needed to sit down to rest his ankle. Shayla pushed her water pouch toward him. "Drink."

"You first," he said.

"I'm okay, but you are hurt. Now drink."

"It's my ankle Shay, I didn't sprain my throat." Mican laughed, but Shayla firmly held the water pouch toward him. He knew not to argue, so he drank. Shayla then turned up the pouch, but saved a sip for Ashton and shoved it in his direction.

Ashton drank the final swallow. "Well, what do we do now? We're out of water."

Mican responded. "What we should have done long before now." He bowed his head and closed his eyes. "Abba, we need your help. It's no surprise to you that I've hurt my ankle and that we're out of water. We ask you to provide for our needs and forgive us for not asking sooner. In the name of your Son. Amen."

When Mican opened his eyes and raised his head, a drop of water hit his nose. "Where did that come from?"

Ashton looked as another drop formed on the tip of the rock directly above Mican's head. "Get your water pouches ready."

Mican scooted out of the way. "This reminds me of the story when Abba provided water from a rock for the Israelites in the wilderness."

The drops came more quickly until it ran like a faucet of fresh, cool water. After filling Shayla's water bag, Ashton handed it to her to tie off, but instead she filled her mouth with a long drink, then handed it to Mican.

Ashton finished refilling Mican's pouch and handed it to Shayla.

Next, he filled his own, then traded places with his sister. While he gulped down a long refreshing drink, she refilled her empty bag. When she stepped back to tie her pouch closed, Ashton finished topping off his bag. When the last drop of water fell, Ashton shouted. "Abba, you're so amazing."

"Yes, he is," said Mican, as he realized the swelling in his foot and ankle had disappeared. "Wow, look." He stood gently and tested it out.

"Careful, big bro," said Shayla.

"Why?" shouted Ashton. "Abba healed it."

Ashton began to jump around and thank Abba for the

water and for healing Mican's ankle. Mican joined him as Shayla stood there in amazement watching her two brothers dance.

"Come on, Shay," yelled Mican and she began to whirl around with her arms stretched out wide.

After several minutes, they had to stop to catch their breath. When they sat down under the now waterless, water faucet, Mican saw the dove. "There you are. Hey, we are glad you are here."

"I am always with you, Mighty One, Abba was pleased when you prayed and more pleased when you praised. You have each grown so much."

Shayla chimed in, "Thank you, Spirit, for bringing us to see the ark. It is one of my favorite stories."

The dove's head slowly lowered and his gaze drifted toward the ground. "It is probably one of the least understood stories people read from Abba's book."

"What do you mean?" asked Ashton.

"People celebrate the ark as God's way to save mankind and animals from the flood, but they fail to realize why it was necessary."

Ashton's forehead crinkled. "Go on."

"After Abba was forced to expel the worship leader from his kingdom, you saw that the fallen ones took daughters of men and formed families with them."

"Yes, we saw that," said Shayla. "It was very upsetting."

"Remember how the women returned to their families with their children?"

They all nodded and Shayla added, "They grew up to be giants."

"Yes, but what you don't realize is that those children—the offspring—the giants—carried the genetic material of the fallen ones. They began to intermingle their DNA with the humans and soon almost all of the population was in some way tainted by them. The people became very violent and corrupt, they practiced a form of mystery religion and sorcery to show their devotion to the fallen ones, their hearts were evil all the time. Only Noah was found pure in Abba's eyes.[ix] That is why he and his family were spared."

All at once, a strange sound began to rise from the valley below. The dove continued. "What you are about to witness will cause you much distress, but you must realize it was done for the good of all mankind. Even most of the animals had to be destroyed because of the wickedness done by the fallen ones."

Mican stood to look over the ridge, Ashton joined

him, but pushed Shayla back.

The dove corrected him. "Let her watch, Mighty One. She needs to learn and understand too."

Shayla stepped between her brothers and stood on a rock. Below them, water began to boil up from underground and rain began to fall.

The dove asked them a question. "Do you realize it had never rained before? When Noah tried to warn the people a flood was coming, they laughed at him."

The last of the animals climbs aboard the ark and the door lifted of its own accord, closing tightly behind them.

"Abba is sealing the door," said the dove, his eyes heavy with sadness.

The water grew deeper, people from the village splashed their way to the ark and pounded on the door.

The dove continued. "Noah could only save his wife, his three sons and their wives who had followed him into the ark, because no one else had believed."

The water rose above the heads of many of the women and children as they clamored to get inside.

Shayla heard their screams, turned her head and placed her hands over her ears. "I've seen enough. Please, can we go now?"

"Before we go, do you know how long Noah and his

family were in the ark?"

"Yeah, forty days," said Shayla.

"That is what most people think, Mighty One, but that is not correct. It rained for forty days and forty nights,[x] but they were in the ark for nearly a year."[xi]

"Wow, I never realized that," said Ashton.

"Yes, Mighty One, they had to wait for the water to recede before they came out. Now, this way please, we must hurry."

They followed the dove back the way they had come. As they grew closer, they could see, at the foot of the mountain, water had begun to rise around the base of the travel arch and the rain now fell harder and harder.

"Run, Shay! Run Ash!"

Small gravel on the slope caused them to slip and slide. They stumbled toward the portal, water reached their ankles, Mican stepped into the archway.

Shayla tumbled and fell into water, but her hand entered the arch and the swirling air pulled her in. Ashton hurled himself at the portal, like doing a running broad jump.

A big slosh of water followed each of them into the tunnel. They tumbled across the fluffy clouds, water splashed over them head-to-toe, then they plopped onto hard sand, their splashes followed and the dry, thirsty soil quickly gobbled up every drop.

Ashton laughed. "I wonder if that is what it feels like to ride on the outside of your car while it goes through the carwash?"

"I don't know," said Mican and he laughed, "but we all needed it."

Shayla laughed too, but her attention turned to their new location. "I wonder where we are now? Didn't we leave Noah's flood? Look, water is rising up to my ankles."

Chapter 9

More Water!

They stood on a wide flat plain, water seeped up, covering their ankles.

"Bubbas, why are we back in water? Didn't we spin away from the flood?"

Mican looked forward and behind. "Run, you two."

"Which way?" yelled Shayla.

Mican waved his hand. "This way! Hurry!"

Ashton and Shayla dashed his direction, but Ashton glanced back. "Wow! Horses and chariots. Where are we?"

"This is not Noah's flood, we are in the Red Sea," yelled Mican.

"Look, the chariots are beginning to bog down," shouted Ashton.

"We need to hurry, before we bog down too," said

Mican.

The water rose up to their knees as they slogged through it. Deeper and deeper, the water rose.

Shayla shouted, "I thought the Israelites went through on dry ground."

"They did," said Ashton, "but we're not Israelites. Keep moving."

"That's true, Ash, not much further. Give me your hand Shay." She reached and took Mican's hand.

It became easier to make progress with him pulling her.

Mican shouted, "Only a few more yards." The water came up to his waist.

"Hurry, Ashy. Do you want to take my hand?"

"No, Shay, I can make it. You just hang onto Mican."

Moments later, Mican climbed onto dry ground with Shayla in-tow. He glanced back and the water was up to Ashton's chin, he was now swimming. "Hurry, dude. Hurry!"

Ashton climbed onto the bank next to his brother and sister. They stared into the distance as the water rose over the heads of the horses. Men and beasts splashed and flailed. It was as if an undertow held them in its grip. The water boiled from their struggle. Finally, it became calm, with no trace of soldiers, horses or chariots.[xii]

Mican laid on his stomach and looked to the horizon. Thousands of men, women and children marched into the desert. "We just survived the flood that killed Pharaoh's army and listen, the people are singing."[xiii]

The dove appeared. "Come Mighty Ones. Time to travel."

They rose and the dove dried their clothes before they solemnly followed him to their next portal. "Through here, please."

Mican faced a narrow slit between two rocks, topped by what looked like a lintel. He held out his hand to his sister, her sad eyes lifted to his. "Ready?"

"I guess so, but we just witnessed the drowning of Pharaoh, his entire army and all of his horses." Tears slipped down her face.

The dove came to comfort her. "Yes, Mighty One. Many people read the story and celebrate the escape of Abba's people, which was wonderful, but few know how heavy his heart was at the loss of all of those Egyptian men. You are feeling the sting of some of that grief."

"Then why did it happen?" she whimpered.

"There are terrible consequences for those who refuse to live by Abba's word. They had to be stopped, little one.

Abba had to rescue his people."

She nodded.

He touched her shoulder with his wing. "In you go, please. May the peace of the King heal your heart."

Sadness covered them, and they entered the arch without much enthusiasm, but this time they bumped and spun before they popped out at the bottom of a hill.

The dove appeared. "This way Mighty Ones. Another stop before you travel again."

Chapter 10

Og of Bashan

More rugged mountains and hot desert sand surrounded them.

"Where are we going?" asked Mican.

"In that direction." The dove pointed and in the distance stood a mountain, frosted with white.

Ashton raised one hand to shade his eyes and stared ahead. After his eyes adjusted to the brightness, his palms leaped up in front of him. "Is that snow?"

"That, Mighty Ones, is Mount Hermon. It has snow on it virtually all year round."

"Are we going to climb all the way to the top?" asked Shayla.

"No, dear one. We will stay on this side and watch what goes on in the valley."

"What's going to happen?" asked Ashton.

"Patience, my friend, you are about to witness a mighty battle between the Israelites and a giant."

Shayla leaned back. "A giant! A live one?"

"Yes, Og of Bashan. He is, or I should say *was* king of his area. His bed was nine cubits by four cubits, which is about thirteen and a half feet long and six feet wide, in your measurements."[xiv]

Shayla glanced at Mican. "Golly, that's more than twice Mican's size, even taller than the skeleton in the cave. That's really scary."

They continued to walk until they reached a point where two armies stood poised below them, one on Mount Hermon, another waiting on the foothills below their perch.

"Bend down and wait, Mighty Ones."

They knelt on the sand, Ashton stretched his body out and crawled to the edge, he rested his chin on his hands. Moments later, a ram's horn sounded and a gigantic person in royal attire walked into the valley from Mount Hermon, accompanied by another large man in battle gear.

Ashton pointed to the valley. "From the way that guy's dressed, he must be the king."

Below their position, a couple of men walked out to

meet the first.

The gigantic man from Mount Hermon lifted his sword high overhead and swung. His blade clashed against the other man's drawn sword, then a battle broke loose.

Men rushed into the fight from both sides. Blood spurted and flowed. Bodies piled up, then came the final death blow, the gigantic man fell forward.

Shayla slid below the ridge. "Yuck, there's blood everywhere, this is gory!"

The dove approached her. "Yes, Mighty One, war is bloody and ugly, not like the video games young people play where the mess stays in one place."

Suddenly, shouts and cheers went up and the northern most group turned and ran.

"Death to Og of Bashan. Og has fallen."[xv]

Ashton jumped up and whooped. "So that is, or was, the thirteen-foot tall giant and we watched him be defeated."

Heads in the valley below turned to look up their hill.

Mican gripped him by the wrist and pulled him out of sight. "Good grief, Ash. The men below heard you."

"Not possible, remember it's already happened in the past." Then he looked at the dove and his eyebrows rose.

"Isn't that right?"

"If something appears in a window or on a screen, then the people on the other side cannot see or hear you, but these people did see you, you were at the battle in the past, not watching it on a screen."

The sounds of men in armor scrambling up the hill reached them.

Ashton's voice rose an octave higher. "I think we need to go now."

The dove flew low to the ground ahead of them. They ran as fast as they could, but when the men topped the ridge, one threw a spear. The sharp object thudded against the stone portal as they stepped through, then instantly spun and floated away. They dropped out at the base of a different hill.

The Spirit appeared. "In this place you will find shelter. Rest here tonight, then travel eastward in the morning. Walk toward the sun, but be careful. Good night, Mighty Ones."

Chapter 11

Into the Sun

"This looks like a good place to take refuge for the night." A dark green palm tree offered shade, clumps of golden amber dates hung from the lower boughs, a small pool of water offered refills for their pouches. A light breeze provided enough coolness to keep them comfortable, but without having to sleep in their jackets. "This is like a tropical vacation," said Mican.

In the morning, as the sun rose, so did the Mighty Ones. They ate breakfast and prepared to get moving. They emerged from beneath their shelter and began their journey eastward.

"It looks like we're going to walk straight into the sun," said Shayla. "I have never seen the sun look so big."

"Shield your eyes," said Mican. "This could get very bright. Walk in my shadow and it will help to shelter you, for a while at least." Mican led, this time Ashton followed next, then Shayla.

Thirty minutes of walking facing the sun, began to take its toll. Mican stopped and turned toward his siblings, his face scorched by the sun. "I need to rest."

Shayla gasped, "Oh Mican." Looking around she spotted shade created by a huge pile of rocks. "Ashy, help me get him over there." They guided Mican to the shelter, Shayla gave her water pouch to him. "Drink!" She emptied her food onto the ground, then drank a sip of water, then poured the rest onto the cloth which had held her food, she placed it on Mican's face.

"Shayla, you shouldn't have."

"Shush," said Shayla. "Lie still."

The coolness of the wet cloth on his face soon had a healing effect, he sat up. "We need to keep moving east."

"We can't," said Ashton. "The sun is too bright. I didn't realize what it was doing to you. I should have known better, dude, I'm sorry."

A strange voice, in a strange language startled them, a young boy with a few goats stood nearby. The boy walked toward them, speaking again, but they couldn't understand him, finally, he motioned with both hands.

"I think he wants us to come with him," said Shayla.

Ashton and Shayla helped Mican to his feet. They slowly walked behind the boy as he ran ahead. They could hear him shouting, then two men rushed toward them. They froze and stiffened, but the men took Mican and placed his arms over their shoulders. "I think they want to help us," said Shayla. As they walked forward, a tent came into view, the men ushered Mican inside.

A very kind-looking woman went in, carrying a bowl filled with cloudy liquid, Shayla and Ashton followed her inside. She began to dab the milky substance on Mican's face. She talked to them, but no one understood. The woman raised her eyes and pointed to the peak of the tent.

Ashton's eyes followed her gaze. "Look guys," and he pointed. Near the peak, they saw a chalky picture of a dove painted on the skins which formed the tent. Ashton looked at the woman and nodded. "Abba's Spirit."

The woman excitedly repeated, "Abba, Abba, Abba."

"I think we are okay here," said Ashton. "Mican you need to rest, bro."

The young boy brought something for them to drink, cloudy like the mixture being applied to Mican's face, Ashton sniffed the cup, then tasted. "It's goat's milk, I think. Different, but not bad." He nodded to the boy.

"Thank you."

After satisfying their thirst, Ashton and Shayla reclined on the sandy floor of the tent close to Mican as he slept for an hour. The sound of a tinkling bell around a goat's neck woke them and Ashton and Shayla sat up.

Mican sat up too and touched his face, which had now dried to a lumpy and crusty texture. Shayla watched him, when he lowered his hands, she laughed. "You look like you're wearing a papier mâché mask.

Ashton leaned forward to see what the fuss was all about and he cackled with laughter. The lady taking care of Mican must have heard them and came in. She moved his hands and pushed them to his side. "No, no, Mighty One."

Ashton laughed again. "I think you have been talking to Abba."

"Jes, jes," replied the woman. "He has given me your languich."

"I see," said Shayla and she laughed too.

"Keep your hands from your face, pease. Lie back and allow me to werk.

Mican laid back again on the folded skins which had cradled his head. The woman used water and a soft cloth to blot Mican's face. "I am Leah. Abba told me to hep you on your journee."

"Thank you very much," said Shayla. "Where are we?"

"You are on the east side of the Reever Jordan, in the mountains of Abarim. Below us is the plain of Moab. Across the reever is the city of Jericho."

Ashton asked, "Do you know what year it is, or how do we know where we are in history."

Unruffled, Leah replied. "The Speerit will show you, rest here until the sun is behind you, then the Speerit will guide you."

"Will Mican be okay?" asked Shayla.

"Jes, jes, he will be fine. Now pease eat, then rest." She handed them a bowl filled with cheese, dates and nuts.

***

A while later, Leah came in with turbans and scarves to cover their faces, she also provided each with a shepherd's robe. "Mighty one, Shayla, your shorts and shirt have proven to be a beet much for the people of my small villege, but Abba has told me of your customs. "Here, my freends. Take these pease. You will need to travel more hidden and these will hep protect you from the sun." Then she worked at splotching something onto their faces.

"What is that," asked Ashton.

Mican sniffed. "It smells like strong coffee, at least I hope that's what it is," and he smiled.

When the solution on their faces dried, she showed Shayla how to tie up her hair, then showed them how to wrap the turbans and sweep the scarves across their faces. "There. You are reedy." Leah handed each of them their full water pouches and their kerchiefs refilled with fresh food.

"Thank you very much Leah. I owe you my life," said Mican as he pressed her small hand between his.

Shayla stepped forward. "May I give you a hug?"

"Certainly, Mighty One Shayla." and she leaned in for a sweet embrace. "Come dis way now."

Leah led them from the tent to the edge of the village, where Mican's two rescuers and the young boy crouched in front of a late afternoon fire.

Mican stepped forward and offered his hand, but both men rose and in turn, gave Mican a kiss on each cheek.

They stepped toward Ashton who tried to wave them off, but—too late—each man kissed him on his cheeks.

Shayla prepared for 'whatever,' but the two men simply bowed in her direction.

Leah couldn't help but laugh as she watched Ashton wipe his face with both hands. "It is a tradeetion of my people, Mighty One Ashton."

"Yeah, tell them thanks for me."

Leah said, "I weell. Now off in dat direction," and she pointed. "When you reech the peak, wait there for the night to pass."

Mican asked, "How will we know which way to go in the morning?"

"The Speerit will guide you. Now go. Stay to the trail until you reech the large boulder, then go to the left of eet. You will reech the peak soon. Abba says to take theese goats with you in case you are seen. The goats will come home in the morning. Blessings, my dear freends."

This time Ashton led the way, followed by five goats. They walked along the trail until they reached the boulder. The path to the left lay hidden by weeds, but they followed Leah's instructions and turned onto it. Soon the peak came into view.

They slowly approached the crest and knelt. In the valley below, thousands of men, women, and children camped on both sides of the Jordan River and surrounded what Leah had told them was Jericho. The night began to deepen and the fires below grew brighter.

Mican pulled his blanket from under his shepherd's robe and decided to settle for the night.

"Mican, what do you think is happening? And who are all those people?" asked Shayla.

"If my Sunday School lessons serve me well, I think they must be the children of Israel encamped around the city wall of Jericho, but I'm not sure which day we have arrived on."

"What do you mean?" asked Ashton.

"Don't you remember? The children of Israel marched around Jericho for six days. Each day they circled the city wall one time, but on the seventh day, they marched around the wall seven times. When they completed the seventh lap, the priests blew the trumpets, then as the men shouted, the wall crumbled into pieces before them."

"So, we are there—I mean here, at that time," said Shayla.

"I guess we will find out tomorrow," said Mican as he rolled over onto his side. The night air had become cool and refreshing. "The sun took a lot out of me, so I'm going to call it a day. Goodnight you two."

A goat had come over to Ashton's side and curled up on the ground near him. Ashton sniffed the air. "Do y'all smell something?"

About that time, Shayla got wind of it. "Shoo-wee. That stinks. Is it that goat?"

"Shooo, scat. Get out of here," said Ashton, but the goat didn't move.

Shayla laughed and joked. "I guess Abba didn't teach the goat English."

Mican rolled halfway back over. "You know I love you two, don't you? In spite of how you smell."

Shayla giggled. "Goodnight, Mican. I love you too and you too Ashy."

Ashton said aloud, "Yeah, yeah, right," but under his breath he whispered, "Love y'all too."

"I heard that," said Mican.

"Me too," giggled Shayla.

Ashton groaned. "Whatever."

***

The next morning, they found themselves awakened by the sun as it marched over the horizon. Mican rolled onto his stomach and crawled toward the ledge. Down below the people stirred. The men on the west side of the Jordan encircled the city wall.

Shayla and Ashton joined their brother and peered into the valley. The goats stood, the male headed toward home, followed by the four females.

"Wow," said Ashton. "I don't see how those female goats can stand the smell of that guy, but they are following right behind them."

Mican teased. "That should give you hope, Ash."

"Yeah, yeah, you are soooo funny, bro."

"By the way, we're all smelling a little rank," said Shayla. "I had forgotten I have my face soap and toothbrush."

"What?" shouted Ashton.

Mican swatted to his side. "Shhhh, knock it off, Ash. This place is like an amphitheater. Your voice will carry."

Ashton whispered, "But Shayla has a toothbrush and soap. We could have used that." Mican turned his head and pursed his lips. "When, Ash? When have we had a chance to wash up?"

"Well we could've in Leah's tent."

Shayla shook her head from side to side and curled her lips. "With all three of us in close quarters, I don't think so, bubba."

Mican crawled away from the ledge and opened his food pouch. "We should probably eat a bite and find some shade. This marching could take a while."

Mican spread his blanket over the scruffy branches of a bush, and there they found refuge from the sun. Later

Mican slipped back to the edge, when he returned he informed his brother and sister of the situation. "We are in luck. It's day seven."

"How can you tell?" asked Shayla.

"I located a guy in the crowd whose turban was unusual. I saw him pass a certain point before we came to sit under this bush. Now he's passed the place again where I first spotted him."

"I have to admit, that is pretty smart, bro," said Ashton.

"What lap are they on?" asked Shayla.

Mican shrugged his shoulders. "Now that, I'm not sure about, but it will take a while for seven laps.

***

The heat had a draining effect on them, so they rested in the shade of Mican's blanket for the remainder of the day. They tried to play 'I Spy,' but everything looked too much the same, so they played tic-tac-toe in the dust to help pass the time. Mican somehow always won.

In the late afternoon, they decided they needed to watch more closely, so they took turns lying on their stomachs and watching over the ridge. On Shayla's turn, she whispered, "Boys, something is happening."

Most of the men had stopped marching, they waited

for the line to finish their last lap, then the priests blew the trumpets. The men had now turned toward the wall and began to shout.

In a loud crash and a burst of dust, the wall of the city fell at their feet, each man walked straight into the city.[xvi]

"Awesome," yelled Ashton.

Shayla added. "Just this minute, we witnessed the fall of the wall of Jericho."

"Which happened thousands of years ago," said Mican with a chuckle.

"Oh yeah, right," said Shayla. Then she asked, "What do we do now?"

Ashton stuck out his hands. "I think we need to pray." They joined together and held hands. He led off. "Dear Abba, we are amazed at all you have shown us. If this is all you desire to show us, we submit to your will, but if there is more, please show us where you want us to go and what we are to do. In the name of your Son. Amen."

When they opened their eyes, Shayla spotted the dove right behind Ashton. "Look Ashy. Your prayer has already been answered."

"Quickly. Gather your things, Mighty Ones."

Mican snatched his blanket from the bush that had been their shade. As he rolled it up he reminded Shayla and Ashton, "Take a drink of water and then secure your pouches and food to your belts. Hurry now."

Only a moment later, they had complied with Mican's instructions, quick as a wink, they were ready to travel again.

Ashton scratched his chin. "I wonder what our next stop will be?"

They hustled toward the dove who waited a few feet ahead of them.

Mican replied, "Let's go see."

This time, a short walk ended with them facing the side of an arch, rather than the front or back entrance.

"This is strange," said Shayla. "Which side do we go to, to enter the arch?"

Chapter 12

Which Way In?

"It depends on where you want to go, Mighty One," replied the dove.

Shayla pushed her hair behind her ear and lifted her shoulders. "Well how should we know where we want to go? I thought Abba wanted us to see certain places and events."

"He does, but sometimes you have a choice," said the dove. "It's like coming to a fork in road. You can either go to the left and climb the hill or go to the right and walk through the valley, but either way you end up at the same place. Now ask yourselves, do you want to go by the mountain passage or through the valley?"

Shayla turned to her brother. "I don't know, Mican, what do you think? You asked the question that got us here."

"Let me see, Shay. The desert was pretty hot and got me sunburned, so—let's take the mountain path. It sounds much cooler." He chuckled and turned toward the dove. "Which way do we enter, Spirit?"

"Step to your left please, then move to face the portal."

They each took two steps, then faced the entrance. Mican reached for Shayla's hand. "Here we go." He stepped in and Ashton rushed to grab Shayla by the wrist, but he missed.

Ashton thought for a second, but Mican and Shayla had already been whisked away, so he jumped head-first in after them.

As they spiraled and spun, Ashton saw Shayla and Mican ahead of him, then they dropped to the ground.

Shayla realized what had happened and reached her free arm back into the whirling vortex, she grabbed Ashton by the ankle, but instead of pulling him out, it jerked her away from Mican's grip and she spun into the tide of clouds again.

***

Mican stood alone on the hillside. Ashton and Shayla had spun off to who-knew-where. He crumpled to his knees. "Abba, I know we failed to stay close as you told us. I'm sorry. Please forgive us for not working harder in following your instructions, but now we need your help. I call upon you and your Spirit to help get us back together and put us on the right track. Please watch over Shay and Ash—and me. Correct this situation for us, please. In the name of your Son. Amen."

Mican looked for shelter, but found none. He curled up on the ground with his back to the base of the travel arch to block the wind and covered himself with his blanket. He finally fell into a fitful sleep, then all of a sudden, he awoke, but remained still.

Two voices drew near.

The first, a deep, raspy voice said, "I am sure they have come to drive us from the land."

"How do you know?" asked the second gruff voice.

"Their book of prophecies foretells it. They have been sent by their King to take the land of Gath."

"But we are so strong and so many, how can they defeat us?"

The voices faded as they turned down the mountainside.

Mican sat up, so this was Gath, the land of the Philistines. Below had to be the valley of Elath, but what time period? Who would have been attacking the giants? Bingo. It had to be when the children of Israel came to take the Promised Land, because we witnessed the fall of Jericho, that started the children of Israel's war west of the Jordan.

He knelt, then shuffled on all fours to the top edge of the mountain, where Mican stretched out on his belly and carefully peeked over to scan the area. He spotted the giants as they crept closer to the campsite of sleeping soldiers on the hillside below.

A wave of panic overtook Mican, but he threw it off as one would throw off a blanket that was too warm. In his spirit echoed the words, 'Sound an alarm,' but how, without being seen? An idea hit him, slide some soil and small pebbles over the crest of the mountain.

Without delay, Mican swished his hand across the ridge, tiny stones and dirt went over the edge and slid. Surely, that wasn't enough. What now? But the tiny pebbles bumped others and they in turn pelted larger rocks, the small action created enough sound to attract the attention of the guards. A trumpet sounded and men scrambled to their feet—the giants were spotted.

Swords clanked, shields thudded, limbs were severed, skin became flayed and hung in horrible strips. The details of the ensuing battle were terrible.

He was glad Shayla hadn't been there to watch, but it

went without saying—giants without heads weren't nearly as tall.

At that very moment, Mican spotted two small dots moving on the opposite ridge. Could it have been? Yep, it was Shayla and Ashton. "Abba Father, how are we going to get back together? I can't go through the valley, while the fighting continues. Please guide us and keep us all safe."

Mican watched as his brother and sister gathered their blankets. Shayla was rolling hers, when Ashton grabbed her hand. With her partially rolled blanket flapping in the wind, he jerked her forward and they both hurtled into an arch.

At once, Mican heard, "Get up, Mighty One." He rose quickly and heard, Run. Faster. Jump," and he hurled himself into a rapidly forming vortex.

He turned and tossed down a pipeline of clouds, amidst wind and flashes of light and darkness, he crashed into something. He caught a glimpse of long, curly hair and snagged it. The ride came to an unexpected stop as they collided with the ground.

"Owww," moaned Ashton.

"Me too," sighed Shayla.

Mican couldn't believe his eyes. "We're back together."

They stood, Shayla threw herself at Mican, he wrapped his arms around her and bent to kiss the curls that had rescued him. "I have never been so glad to see anyone in my life as I am to see you two."

Mican pushed his sister out to arms-length and stared into her eyes, "Shayla Marie, I was afraid I had lost you and I would never have the opportunity to tell you what a loving and sweet sister you are. And to tell you how much I love you." He gave her another hug, kissed her head again, then turned toward Ashton.

Ashton saw him coming. "Come on dude, you're not gonna give me a kiss, are you?"

Shayla laughed, but Mican walked straight up to him. "Ash, since the day you were brought home from the hospital, I've never had a day alone. I used to think that was awful, but now I know it was a gift. It took being totally alone for me to learn it, but you are a gift." He tipped his head. "You haven't always been easy to get along with," he chuckled, "but you are an amazing brother. The way you now listen to and obey the Spirit is awesome to watch. And I love you, man."

Ashton surprised even himself when he flung his arms

toward Mican to give him a hug. "You too, man. No one could ask for a better brother." Then he cut his eyes toward Shayla. "And no one had better repeat a word of this."

Shayla giggled. "I promise," then she wrapped her arms around both of her brothers.

After resting and eating a bite, Ashton shared Shayla's ideas with Mican. "While we were separated and it was getting dark, we needed to find shelter, but looking around, I couldn't see anything but hills and rock."

Mican nodded, "I had the same problem."

"Then Shay had this amazing idea. She thought that we should put her blanket over two rocks that were close together and weigh the blanket down with smaller rocks; then we could put my blanket down the back to close the end where the wind wouldn't come through, we'd use our shepherds' cloaks like blankets and use our turbans like pillows."

Mican turned to her. "My, my! Our little sister has a big brain. Good for you Shay. I'm proud of you."

"Thanks, but all I can say is, I was trained by the best."

Mican cocked his head to the side and his eyebrows scrunched together.

She explained. "I got the idea from you using your

blanket as a shade covering and from yours and Ashy's forts in the den."

Mican laughed. "Thank goodness Mom didn't have to clean up all of those messes for nothing." Then he looked around. "Where do you think we are now? Or should I ask, when are we here?"

Ashton and Shayla both knew exactly what he meant.

"Maybe we need to pray," said Shayla.

Mican didn't even hesitate, he reached for their hands. "Thank you, Father for keeping us safe and for bringing us back together. Only you could have done such a wonderful thing. Now, we would like to know the next step of your plan for us. Please let us know your will. In the name of your Son. Amen."

When they opened their eyes, the Spirit hovered in the middle of their circle. "Mighty Ones, the Sabbath begins at sundown and Abba wishes for you to rest. You have had a hard journey thus far. There," and he pointed, "take your blankets and other wares to that tree at the base of the cliff for shelter and I will stay with you for a while."

***

They did exactly as he had directed and found a small spring bubbling up near the base of the tree. Night fully arrived, but the moon lit the landscape. The warm breeze swirled around them.

Shayla had another idea. "Boys, I would like to wash up a bit. Can we make a bath area?"

Mican placed his hand under his chin with one finger resting on his cheek. "Hmmm, I think we can do that, will a fort-style-bath be okay?"

Shayla smiled. "I'm sure any kind of bath will be okay."

"Help me, Ash." The boys used their hands to dig a shallow area which filled with water and which could be used like a bathtub. The warm sand heated the cool spring water. Mican tied a blanket to the tree and stood with his back to Shayla as she pulled out her washcloth, soap, toothbrush and paste.

She started with brushing her teeth. She spattered toothpaste on the blanket as she spoke. "My goodness, I can't believe how good a toothbrush feels after several days of not brushing."

"Why am I holding this blanket if all you're doing is brushing your teeth?" asked Mican.

"You never mind, mister, and keep holding, I'm washing up too."

"Oh heavens, no details," laughed Ashton. "Women and their bathing rituals."

Shayla ooo-ed and ahhh-ed over the feel of fresh, clean water and the warm sand. After several minutes Mican laughed. "Hurry up, Shay, my arm is falling asleep. I'm afraid it's going to drop off."

"Okay, I'm all done."

Mican lowered the blanket. "Why are your clothes wet?"

"I didn't want to put on dirty clothes after I'd washed off. They will dry soon enough in this breeze." Then she shouted, "Okay, who's next?"

"Shay, I know this is an imposition," Mican put his hands together, tipped his head a little and gave her a cheesy grin, "but can we use your toothbrush? Pleeeeease."

Shayla hadn't thought of that, but Mican laced his fingers together, dropped onto one knee in front of her and pitifully repeated some of her words. "I can't even imagine how good a toothbrush would feel, after several days of not brushing." Then he broadened his cheesy grin.

Shayla burst out laughing. "Okay, but you two owe me."

Ashton grabbed the toothbrush. "Me, first."

So Mican snatched the soap and lathered his hands. Rubbing his face, he realized whatever stain Leah had put on him was beginning to wash off.

Shayla laughed "Your face is streaky."

"Okay, Miss Smarty. A little privacy please." He lifted the corner of the blanket and shoved it toward her.

Shayla playfully gripped the corner and turned her back.

After some much-needed splashing and some sighs of relief, the boys finished, Shayla's clothes had dried and everyone settled down for a meal of dried meat, fruit, and nuts.

The Spirit waited for his charges to nestle into their blankets for the night.

The moon drowsily lit their surroundings, Mican scooched under his blanket and asked a question. "Spirit, why are there giants here if the flood was meant to destroy them?"

Chapter 13

The Tower

The dove inhaled a deep breath, his eyes saddened and he began to tell the story. "After the flood, when the wives of the sons of Noah began baring children, Ham's wife secretly taught her son Cush [xvii]and later her grandson Nimrod, the mystery religion of the fallen ones."

Mican wrinkles his forehead. "I never realized that Nimrod was Noah's great grandson."

"Yes, and the wives carried a small amount of the genetic material of the giants which was passed on to their children, but that DNA was inactive until it was blended with the magic she taught her son and grandson, that combination of the DNA and mystery religion revived the line of the giants. Many people think because Nimrod was a large man who *stood before Abba*, that it meant he was a good man, but that is not true. In the story, when he stood 'before' Abba, the Hebrew word actually meant he stood *against* Abba."[xviii]

"Oh dear," said Shayla.

The dove nodded in agreement. "Yes, Shayla. Do you remember the story of the tower of Babel? The beginning of Nimrod's kingdom was at Babel where the tower was built. Nimrod told his people that they were going to build a tower to reach the heavens.[xix] He planned and took steps to reach Abba by human works, as a result, much rebellion and witchcraft arose in that place."

The dove stroked the air with his wing. "Observe."

A large window frame appeared. The area where the glass should have been, became white and frosty. An image appeared. A large, broad man stood on a platform, he held his hands out facing a throng of tanned faces. "My people, we shall build this tower to reach heaven. We shall bring ourselves face-to-face with God. We shall be as God."

The scene changed and scanned the crowd. Thousands of people knelt before him and began to sway and chant. Next, the tower came into view, they could see the sound from the chanting crowd, spiraled upward. At the unfinished top of the tower, a dark cloud formed and a portal opened. The cloud began to rotate around the top of the tower.

As the darkness moved and swirled, it got faster and faster, Shayla screamed and pointed. "Boys, look! It's those awful creatures that were around Abba's castle. They're coming through a hole in the sky above the tower."

Ashton pointed. "Look at 'em. The louder their chanting gets, the bigger the hole gets over the tower." The scene switched to the crowd. "And look at the people, their swaying is getting wilder. They're crashing into each other, they look like they're drunk!"

Shayla screamed. "The louder they chant and the wilder they sway, the drunker they look."

Mican stared in amazement. "And their chanting and swaying are in rhythm with the swirling of the fallen ones, the faster the people chant and sway, the faster the creatures swarm."

Hideous screams fell toward the crowd and fueled their excitement.

Shayla drew her hands over her hears. "Stop it! Make it stop, Spirit."

With the swish of his wing, the fierce noise and violent activity vanished.

Shayla leaned against Mican. "Oh bubba, that was awful."

"Shay-belle, you're trembling. Remember, it was in the past and they couldn't see you."

"I know, but it was still terrible. To think they were chanting to those creatures—it was awful."

Ashton placed his hand on Shayla's shoulder. "I understand now why Abba confused their language.[xx] Their behavior was very ungodly, I could even feel a magnetic-like pull. I understand how people could be drawn into it, especially if they don't know Abba personally."

Mican leaned Shayla up straight. "I could feel it too, Ash."

Shayla wiped her face. "Really, Mican?"

"Oh yeah, Shay. I could feel it." He stared into her eyes. "So, does that mean you could feel it too?"

"Yes, that was why I was so scared. I felt the pull on my mind and my body." She started to cry. "I thought it was just me. I thought that maybe I was evil or something." She wept uncontrollably.

Mican wrapped his arm around his sister again, but it was the Spirit's words that brought her comfort.

"No sweet child. You are not evil. It is the power of

the fallen ones that chases after the sweet and innocent, people like you. It would be quite a victory for them if they could lure someone like you away from Abba. That is why Ashton felt it too. Mican, you *sensed it*, but you didn't *feel it* like your brother and sister did. You are older, stronger and have known Abba longer than they have."

Shayla dried her tears. "Thank you, Spirit. I was so afraid that I was not good enough."

"Sweet lady, you should know by now that it is not about how good you are. It is about what the Son has done for you and about you asking for forgiveness when you fail."

Shayla sniffed, "You are right. I should know that. The power that the fallen ones can have on a person's mind is scary."

"Again, sweet lady, that is why you must grow in Abba's word, so the words of the King become more real in your mind than the words of the enemy."

Shayla nodded, but it was Ashton who answered. "That is a good lesson, Spirit. Thank you very much."

The dove continued his story. "Nimrod lived in the land of Shinar. It was also from there that a person named, Asshur went out and built Nineveh,[xxi] which became a very wicked city.[xxii] Much evil was done there and the genes of the giants reactivated there too."

Mican rubbed his chin. "I remember that Abba wanted Jonah to go to Nineveh to tell the people that they should turn from their wickedness or they would be destroyed."

"Yes," said the dove. "Jonah wanted no part of it because those people were so cruel, they had even skinned people alive."

Ashton gasped. "Really? That's not just a saying?"

"No, it was actually practiced by the Ninevites. Remember, Jonah ended up in the belly of the big fish.[xxiii] When he was spat out onto the shore, people who saw it ran into town to tell everyone. What most people don't know is that the god of Nineveh was Dagon, a half-fish and half-man deity,[xxiv] so when people saw Jonah vomited up by a fish[xxv] they ran to share the news. And when he walked into town with his skin bleached from stomach acid, smelling like fish, the people were ready to believe him."

"Wow, that explains a lot," said Mican.

Shayla added. "It really does, but I have another question about Nimrod."

"Yes, Mighty One."

"Was Nimrod a giant?"

"Well, he was a very large man, so you could say he was the beginning of the resurgence of the giants," explained the Spirit. "Not only was he of impressive stature, he promoted the mystery religion. That is what you witnessed at the tower."

Shayla tilted her head. "I don't remember hearing much about any giants, except Goliath. Did King David kill Goliath *because* he was a giant?"

The dove swiped his wing in the air again. "Let's take a look."

A window opened, and frosted-over, a sandy battlefield appeared. On one side of a valley, the army of Israel stood, across the valley, at the foot of the opposite mountain loomed the Philistine army.[xxvi] One man in the front stood head and shoulders taller than his companions.

The dove pointed. "That is Goliath of Gath. He is over fifteen feet tall."[xxvii]

Ashton noticed his fine armor. "Look, his helmet looks like polished brass, he's wearing a chainmail coat and those things on his legs are called greaves. They look like they're made of brass too."[xxviii]

Mican's face pulled tight and he stared at the ground. "If I remember right, this is the valley of Elah."[xxix]

The dove turned to Mican. "Very good, Mighty One."

"But which day are we in the valley?" asked Mican.

Ashton lifted his shoulders and spread his hands. "What do you mean, bro?"

"Well, I think they were there about forty days, with old loud-mouth over there, taunting the Israel army every day."[xxx]

"Yes, Mighty One, you are correct, but watch for a moment."

They heard the giant cry out. "Why don't you choose one man to come out against me. If he wins, we," and he swept his arm toward the Philistine warriors, "we will follow your king Saul, but if I win, you will be our servants."[xxxi]

A skinny, young boy wandered into view. He approached the king's men with supplies.[xxxii]

Mican shouted, "That must be David."

Shayla looked at him with her nose wrinkled. "Gee, bubba, are you sure. He looks about my age."

"Sure, Shay. Remember he was only a boy when this happened. He wasn't the king yet."

"Oh, okay, but…."

The dove interrupted. "Mighty Ones, watch David."

Goliath shouted again. "I defy the armies of Israel.

Send out one man, that I may fight him. If I win, you will become our slaves, but if he wins, we will serve your king."[xxxiii]

David heard the Philistine and walked to the edge of the battlefield and lifted his voice to Goliath. "Who should stand against the army of the living God?"

A messenger sent word to the young lad. "King Saul wishes to speak with you."[xxxiv]

David followed the soldier.

Saul examined David's youthful face. "You are only a boy and cannot defeat this giant."

David bent his head toward the ground. "But Sir, while I watched my father's sheep, I killed a lion and a bear. I rescued a lamb from the mouth of each. The Lord delivered me from them, shall he not also deliver me from this unclean Philistine."[xxxv]

The dove whispered, "Notice, Mighty Ones, this was not David's first fight. Abba had been growing him in strength, but also training him in strength of heart. Then King Saul tried to arm David with his armor, it didn't fit."[xxxvi]

The dove continued. "David knew his strengths and knew the weapons he had trained with, he walked to a brook and chose five smooth stones. Notice that he didn't run, he was following *my* directions. He placed the stones in his pouch and carried his sling in his hand.[xxxvii] When he walked out to meet the Philistines, Goliath shouted at him, do you think I'm a dog? Then he made a big mistake. He cursed David by the Philistine gods."[xxxviii]

"What did David do?" asked Shayla.

"Watch."

David told Goliath, "You come to me with your sword and shield, but I come to you in the name of the Lord of our army, the God of Israel's army, that is who you are defying. The Lord is going to deliver you into my hands, because the battle belongs to him."[xxxix]

Mican, Shayla, and Ashton's attention was riveted to the window.

Goliath stepped into the valley, walking toward David.

David rushed out to meet him, put his hand in his bag and pulled out a stone. He placed the smooth rock into his sling and spun it. He released. The stone flew out and struck Goliath in the forehead, sinking in deep. The giant toppled like a statue with his face to the ground.

David had no sword of his own, so he ran to the Philistine and stood on his body, pulled Goliath's sword from its sheath and chopped off the giant's head. The

Philistine army turned and fled.[xl]

The image faded and the window closed.

The dove fluttered in front of them. "As you saw, David did not kill Goliath because he was a giant. He killed Goliath because he was disrespecting David's God, Abba, your God also. Giants never have respect for Abba, because they were the creation of the Fallen Ones who were deliberately defying God's law."

"Can't they repent," asked Ashton.

"No, Mighty One, they cannot because of their polluted DNA.

Shayla turned toward the Spirit again. "So, were there many giants beside Goliath? I haven't ever heard anyone talking about any giant, but him."

"That is because many people have little understanding of the subject," said the dove.

"Along with not understanding, I think many teachers would be afraid they would be accused of teaching heresy," said Mican. "It's a pretty far-out subject."

"What is heresy?" asks Shayla.

"It's false teaching, Shay. It's something that is contrary to the regular line of religious belief." Then he looked to the dove. "Isn't that right?"

The Spirit agreed with Mican. "Good job, Mighty

One, but I might add that the 'regular lines of religious belief' as you put it, should always line up with Abba's words."

The Spirit continued to address Shayla. "I agree that it is an unusual subject, but there are many examples. If you look at the words of Samuel, in his second book, you see two giants are named there. They are Ishbibenob[xli] and Saph.[xlii]"

"Who?" Shayla laughed, "That first one's a mouthful."

"It's pronounced in the Hebrew, yish·vo'veh nove, in your language the v's would sound like b's. Ish-bo'beh-nob."

"That's still a mouthful," said Shayla and she laughed again.

"That is true, Mighty One, but Samuel also referred to the brother of Goliath[xliii] and another giant with six fingers and six toes on each hand and foot.[xliv] Those were the sons of a giant at Gath. Two of them were the giants that you saw fall in that last battle, Mican."

He bobbed his head. "Hmmm, okay."

"Then, Mighty Ones, in the first book of The Chronicles of the Kings, a giant named Sippai[xlv] is mentioned. Passages in the books of Numbers and

Deuteronomy also discussed giants. There were many, many giants in the land. The children of Israel had to take the land by force. The giants had to be killed to take the Promised Land."

"Do you remember in the book of Numbers when Moses sent out twelve spies?"[xlvi] asked the dove.

"I remember that," said Ashton.

"Ten of the twelve spies came back telling Moses the land truly flowed with milk and honey, but they also gave a bad report when they talked about the sons of Anak, who were giants. They reported that the people were like grasshoppers in the sight of those people.[xlvii] Only Joshua and Caleb came back with a good report.[xlviii] They knew Abba was with them and told Moses they should go up immediately because they would be able to defeat the giants of the land."

"I never thought about it in that way," said Ashton.

"And do you recall the number of times Abba told Joshua to 'be strong and courageous'? Do you know why the King said that?"

Heads wagged side-to-side.

"They were being sent to wage war against the people of the land who had allowed giants to rise up again. The warriors were told, in many cases to leave no one alive.

That was because the DNA of the fallen ones had been passed on through marriages and having children. The whole population of the area had become unclean again. Abba didn't hate the people, but they had allowed the mystery religion and the DNA of the fallen ones to pollute their people. It had to be stopped or the whole earth would have been polluted again."

Ashton added, "I can totally understand now, why the Lord reminded Joshua over and over again to be strong and of good courage. He was being sent on a very hard mission."

"Yes, Mighty One, Abba was with Joshua, but wanted him to learn to see with his spirit and not with his eyes only."

"I can see that now. Thank you for the lesson," replied Shayla.

"Sleep now, Mighty Ones, for tomorrow you will see a giant."

Chapter 14

The Shock

When Mican awoke, he found a line, drawn in the dust with an arrow tip pointing the way. His laughter woke Shayla and Ashton.

Ashton stretched and yawned. "What's so funny, bro?"

Mican pointed to the ground.

His brother realized the fun of it and laughed too.

Shayla couldn't see past her brothers until she stood. "Why is that so funny? It's only directions the Spirit drew." Then she laughed too. "How did he do that? With his beak? Or his wing? I guess it is funny now that I think about it."

Mican glanced at his sister. "We need to get ready to move. Any chance of using your toothbrush Shay?"

"Okay, but me first." She took a sip of water from her

pouch and plunged the paste filled brush into her mouth. "Man, this is nice. I never knew how great brushing your teeth feels." She scrubbed softly, then spat toothpaste into the sand and rinsed her mouth with another sip and spat again. "Ahhhh."

Mican took the toothbrush and splashed a little water from his pouch onto it to rinse away Shayla's leftover toothpaste.

Ashton and Shayla took turns washing their faces in the tub area. Over his shoulder, Mican shouted, "Fill your water bags from the spring. I don't know how far we have to go before we whirl again."

They both drank freely from their water pouches, then took turns dipping the bags into the spring.

"Don't stir up the sand, Ashy. I don't want grit in my water."

"Okie dokie, little Mighty One." Ashton grinned. "Get Mican's pouch and we can fill it for him while he washes his face."

While carefully filling Mican's pouch, Shayla realized she was hungry. "Guys, we should have eaten before we brushed our teeth."

"No time now, Shay-Belle. We need to pack up and move. I feel a *push* in my spirit to get on our way. We can munch as we walk."

Shayla smiled at her oldest brother. "Okay, we can do that."

After rolling their blankets and dressing in their shepherd's cloaks and turbans, they headed in the direction of the arrow. They walked for two hours before Mican spotted a message written in the sand. He read it aloud, "Stop here and rest."

"Woohoo," said Shayla. "Just in the nick of time. I'm bushed."

"I'm a little tired myself," said Ashton.

They pulled out their water pouches and sat in the shade of an olive tree. Ashton decided to turn with his feet up the hill with his head downhill.

"What are you doing Ashy?"

"I thought I would lessen the chance of my feet swelling."

"You look like Aunt Martha propping her feet up on the back of the sofa." She and Mican both laughed.

"Well it actually feels good, O' Mighty laughing Ones." Ashton glanced at them and grinned.

The dove arrived and piped in. "Good for you, Ashton. Getting more blood and oxygen to your brain, I see."

Shayla gave him a sharp look. "Really? Should I do

that?"

"No time now, Mighty One. We need to move. Today is a special day."

"What makes it special, Spirit?" asked Shayla.

The dove faced her, his eyes were moist and stared downward. "The time has come for more revelation, dear one. Take a sip of water, but not too much."

They complied with the instruction.

"Now through there please," and the Spirit pointed to the narrowest arch they had seen yet.

Mican rubbed his chin. "Will we fit through there?"

"Yes, Mighty One, it will be tight, but narrow is the way."[xlix]

Mican took the lead. Once in the portal, thunder erupted around them and the whirlwind darkened. They bumped and skimmed across the cloud, then the darkness faded. They dropped out of the travel circle at the base of a hill. They looked all around for the dove, but he was nowhere to be seen. The sun sank into the horizon, but enough light remained to enable them to search their surroundings.

Mican, alert as usual, pointed at the ground. "Look at the number of footprints over there. Something very important must have drawn a large crowd to this place.

Most of the crowd stood over there." Mican pointed, then his gaze drifted up the slope of the hill.

Without a word, his siblings did the same. Their faces softened and saddened. On the hill, lit from behind by the setting sun, stood three crosses, stained and dripping with thick clots of blood.

Finally, able to choke out words, Mican said, "This hill is Golgotha, the place of the crucifixion of Abba's Son."

Shayla buried her face in Ashton's shoulder. "Oh Ashy. This is too horrible."

Ashton turned his head and tilted his chin down onto the top of Shayla's head. "It is so hard to understand why he would die in our place, for our sins," then a tear dripped onto his sister's hair.

Mican stepped over and wrapped his arms around both of them. "But Abba's Son did, and all people have to do is to truly believe it in their hearts, then ask him to forgive them and ask Him to be Lord of their life. I'm glad that we've all done that."

Shayla wiped her face. "Now I know why it got so dark in the portal. That must have been when he died."

Ashton added, "And why the travel arch was so narrow, remember, narrow is the way that leads to life."

They stood for several minutes until the Spirit returned. They heard a tender whisper, "This way, Mighty Ones. It is time to go." The dove led them in silence to the far end of the hill. "Mighty Ones, this will be your final *slide*, shall we say, at least for this adventure."

Mican's eyes filled with tears and he stepped toward the dove. "Before we go, Spirit, I have a question."

"Yes, Mican, what is it?"

"When we saw the fallen ones kidnap the women, I told Shayla not to worry because it was all in the past, it was over, but I heard in my spirit, 'Is it, my son? Is it over? Is it all in the past?' Why did Abba say that? What did he mean?"

As night descended on them, the dove sighed and answered. "Because, Mighty One, it is not all over."

"What?" cried Shayla. "What do you mean it's not over?"

"Because, dear one, the giants are surfacing again in your day."

"How can that be?" asked Ashton.

"The same way they were brought back after the flood, Mighty One. Mankind has once again started practicing the mystery religion, and has begun tampering with the DNA of people and animals. Have you not been aware of the increase in popular movies and television shows that have witchcraft in them? And there are shows that make it seem good, even enjoyable and romantic to marry vampires, werewolves and the like?"

Ashton nodded.

The dove continued, "Even in some of the superhero shows and the shows that depict people with special powers, many of the characters have been altered and made genetically different. These shows are preparing young people to mentally accept the false religion and preparing young women to accept relationships with hybrids, which Abba has expressly forbidden. They are making it appealing to be chosen, as a mate, by chimera, which are creatures with mixed or altered genes."

"Wow, that's alarming," said Ashton. "I've never thought of them that way. I just thought they were fantasy stories."

"They are not fantasy, Ashton, and they are being made for a reason. Maybe some of the actors and directors don't realize the enemy's purpose for these movies, but they have a purpose, they are to prepare a generation to accept the next arrival of the giants."

Chapter 15

The Fourth Industrial Revolution

The dove made another shocking revelation. "In addition to giants, vampires, zombies, and animal-human hybrids, you should be prepared to resist what is being called, the Fourth Industrial Revolution. The Industrial Revolution brought in the use of machines to increase productivity and decrease the labor required to produce crops and products, but this new phase will try to merge human's with technology."

Mican straightened. "I think I read about that. An article I read talked about implanting a phone chip, so you can simply think about calling someone and they get called."

"Yes, the new Artificial Intelligence, known as A.I., will be a springboard for that technology. First, they created a robot that can think for itself, then they implant the A.I. with awareness of itself, or sentience. Next, they will name it Tom or something human-sounding, then they will say he has a soul because he is self-aware, when anyone tries to argue against that notion, the idea will be proposed that the one arguing doesn't have a soul either so it doesn't matter."

Ashton rubs his chin. "Gees Louise. How do we argue against that?"

"Only Abba and I can give you the words, when the time comes, but be sure to pray and ask. Now that the first generation of A.I. is behind us, its creators are experimenting with combining their technology with humans. That includes the article you read Mican."

Shayla swished her curls. "Will they be able to do that? That reminds me of that creepy show about the Borg." She held out her hands in front of her and walked like a zombie. "'Resistance is fu-tile.' That creeped me out."

"Yes, Shayla, they will have some degree of success, but Abba will not tolerate their meddling for long. Just like with abortions, Abba has tried to change the minds of people, but some are so hard-hearted, they will not listen. Abba can only hold off punishment for so long."

Shayla bristled. "You mean Abba will punish women

who have had abortions?"

"Not if they are repentant, but the powers that promote the killing of unborn babies will, in time be punished, just as the Israelites where taken captive by oppressors for sacrificing their children to Baal, so too will your country be punished, if the people do not repent."[l]

Mican said, "This isn't looking very good for our nation, is it?"

"You are right, Mighty One, there are some hard times ahead."

Ashton asked, "What else do we need to know about?"

The dove suddenly shivered. "I must also warn you to be aware of the coming public announcement that aliens are real."

Mican shook his head. "No way."

"Unfortunately, these aliens will claim to be gods, and will be able to produce many miracles and supernatural events, but they are, in truth, the Fallen Ones. Remember when Moses performed miracles as directed by Abba? Pharaoh's magicians were able to do some of the same acts."[li]

Mican's face tightened. "I remember that, I wondered why Abba didn't stop them."

"Because Mican, they had the supernatural abilities

given to the Fallen Ones by Abba, he did not take those away when they were cast out of the Kingdom. When you expressed an interest in understanding the giants of old, you and your siblings were permitted to take this journey, but now you must pray, dear ones. You have a great challenge ahead of you. Now, as I said, it is time for you to return."

Ashton asked, "Don't stop there, what kind of challenge?"

"Now that you know the truth, Mighty One, when these things take place, it will be your responsibility to share the truth with others. It will not be easy. You will be mocked and even hated by some for your beliefs."

Shayla cringed. "Now I'm afraid."

The dove fluttered toward her, rested one wing on her shoulder. "But Mighty One, you know as long as you stay close to Abba there is nothing to be afraid of, so never allow your relationship with the King to grow cold."

"Okay, I'll remember," said Shayla.

The dove unfolded one more warning and laid it at their feet. "In addition to the challenge of sharing your faith, you need to know that there will be another coming attack."

Mican leaned toward the dove. "What type of 'coming

attack'?"

"A plague will be unleashed upon the world. It will bring social breakdown and economic breakdown. You will be bombarded by people's opinions of what is happening and what to do, but you must rely on Abba and me for guidance. Again, Mighty Ones, we will be with you and give you wisdom, but do not treat the plague lightly, also do not fear it. Take care to protect yourself, but ultimately it is up to us to protect you. Know this, in the same way you wouldn't jump off a cliff and say, 'Abba will protect me,' you cannot charge ahead recklessly. Use common sense, but more importantly, use *Abba-sense* to protect yourself."

Mican looked at his brother and sister and they nodded. "We will, Spirit. We understand."

"Along with this plague will come cries of, 'Where is your God?' People's hearts will turn cold, but do not be shaken, there will come a great falling away.[lii] But it must be so."

Shayla squirmed and her face reflected a struggle. "Spirit, why will people fall away, if we are trying so hard to get them to believe in Abba?"

"Good question, dear one. Many in the church today are like Ashton was, before he saw his sin and called on the King to save him. Because they are religious and attend church, many believe they are followers of Abba, but they are not, not truly in their hearts. There is a passage in Abba's book that explains this, in his Son's own words."

> Not everyone that says unto me, Lord, Lord, shall enter into the kingdom of heaven; but he that doeth the will of my Father which is in heaven.
>
> Many will say to me in that day, Lord, Lord, have we not prophesied in thy name? and in thy name have cast out devils? and in thy name done many wonderful works?
>
> And then will I (Abba's Son) profess unto them, I never knew you: depart from me, ye that work iniquity.[liii]

"Those people will fall away when the life of following Abba becomes difficult."

Mican asked, "How can we get them back?"

"Well, Mighty One, those may be the hardest people to reach. They will believe they did everything right and that Abba let them down. That will be next to impossible to un-do."

Shayla shrugged. "So, what do we do?"

"In truth, you try to reach as many as you can, but there will come a great persecution against the church. At that time, you will need to teach those who remain faithful to the King, how to be strong and resist the urge to fall away."

Shayla groaned, "It all seems so impossible."

"In your own power, it is my dear. It may be awhile yet before you face this part of the challenge and it's true that it will be difficult, but it will not be impossible. You need to stay in Abba's word, that is where part of your strength will come from. And remember, Abba loves you very much and wants to spend time with you every day."

Mican surveyed the faces of his siblings. "We will remember, Spirit."

The dove nodded. "Now, if you are ready."

Shayla asked, "Spirit, we've been gone for a week. When—and where—will we end up when we return?"

"You will be back at Chaco Canyon, in time to return to camp," replied the Spirit. "Hold hands, Mighty Ones, it's time to take another leap of faith."

Chapter 16

Comfort

Mican smiled and firmly gripped Shayla's hand. He waited to be sure Ashton took hold of the other. "Ready? Remember to bend your knees. Here we go," and he stepped into the swirling center of the portal.

Mican popped out of the archway in time to hear Bailey's plea to Dr. Lightfoot. "Honestly Dr. L., I don't see them anywhere. We need to go back and look for them."

"Bailey, I'm sure they will be here any minute." Dr. Lightfoot turned and headed to the van.

"But Dr. L., I'm serious, one minute they were standing there, and the next minute they were gone. It looked like Shayla got sucked through a straw and into space. Ashton caught her by the arm and he got slurped in too. Then Mican grabbed Ash-boat by the leg and it whooshed him away."

Shayla stepped through the arch in time for this part of the conversation.

Dr. Lightfoot plopped his fists at the waist of his lean frame. "Bailey, enough! You are always trying to stir up some kind of trouble."

"This time, I'm not, I promise. And when we first got here, that Medicine Man was talking to them. Could he have—I don't know—," she twists one hand like a tornado going up, "spirited them away somehow?"

"Look Bailey, what you are saying is impossible. I'm sure they have already started back to the bus. Mican is very responsible. Now let's go. Move it."

Ashton stumbled out of the whirlwind and stood next to his brother and sister, as the vortex closed, a whoosh of air pushed Bailey's hair around her face, she spun to discover Ashton, Shayla, and Mican standing by a stone archway. Her mouth fell open.

Shayla and Mican walked past and Shayla said, "I've never seen you speechless before, Bailey. You'd better come with us."

Covering the distance between Bailey and the van took only seconds.

Dr. Lightfoot spotted Mican and Shayla wearing their shepherd's cloaks and turbans and leaned out of the van. "See Bailey, they've been at the gift shop. Now come on, I'm tired of your shenanigans."

Mican stood at the van door and watched as Ashton placed his hands against Bailey's back and pushed just a little. "Come on Bailey, you're holding up the van and I'm ready to get back to the comforts of camp."

Bailey's arms dangled at her sides as she shuffled along in front him. "Comforts? Of camp? You guys are nuts. You're all weird."

They reached the door of the van and Ashton said, "Now Bailey, we've already had that discussion earlier this morning."

Right before they stepped onto the bus, Mican saw the dove flash past the door, the white feathers caught Bailey's attention.

She looked into the sky. "Was that a dove?"

Dr. Lightfoot shouted, "Bailey, enough. Now get on the bus."

Mican laughed as he reached the back seat.

Ashton watched as he made the gesture for 'drop the mic.'

The End?

Not Even Close

Author Bio

June Whatley has taught first through third grades in a Christian school; she has also taught Middle Graders in two different Christian schools; and has taught Study Skills in the Remedial Developmental Department of the third largest college in Tennessee.

Mrs. Whatley holds a combination Master of Arts degree in Counseling and Education from Regent University in Virginia Beach, Virginia.

June is a wife, mother and grandmother of four of the greatest Grands in history.

Endnotes

---

[i] Brian Breland, Thanks, bubba.
[ii] From book one, *The Sleeper Awakens*.
[iii] *The Sleeper Awakens*.
[iv] Isaiah 14:12.
[v] Isaiah 14:12.
[vi] Genesis 6:1-2.
[vii] Genesis 6:4.
[viii] Genesis 6:4.
[ix] Genesis 7:1.
[x] Genesis 7:4.
[xi] Genesis 7:11 & 8:13.
[xii] Exodus 14:25-30.
[xiii] Exodus 15.
[xiv] Deuteronomy 3:11.
[xv] Deuteronomy 3:3.
[xvi] Joshua 6:20.
[xvii] Genesis 10:8.
[xviii] Genesis 10:8-9.
[xix] Genesis 11:4.
[xx] Genesis 11:6-7.
[xxi] Genesis 10:11.
[xxii] Jonah 1:2.
[xxiii] Jonah 1:17 & 2:10.
[xxiv] Dagon, a Philistine deity of fertility; represented with the face and hands of a man and the tail of a fish. Strong's Concordance, H1712, A.

[xxv] Jonah 2:10.
[xxvi] 1 Samuel 17:3.
[xxvii] 1 Samuel 17:4.
[xxviii] 1 Samuel 17:5-6.
[xxix] 1 Samuel 17:2.
[xxx] 1 Samuel 17:16.
[xxxi] 1 Samuel 17:8-9.
[xxxii] 1 Samuel 17:17-18.
[xxxiii] 1 Samuel 17:10.
[xxxiv] 1 Samuel 17:31.
[xxxv] 1 Samuel 17:34-36.
[xxxvi] 1 Samuel 17:38.
[xxxvii] 1 Samuel 17:40.
[xxxviii] 1 Samuel 17:43.
[xxxix] 1 Samuel 17:43-46.
[xl] 1 Samuel 17:48-51.
[xli] 2 Samuel 21:16-17.
[xlii] 2 Samuel 21:18.
[xliii] 2 Samuel 21:19.
[xliv] 2 Samuel 21:22.
[xlv] 1 Chronicles 20:4.
[xlvi] Numbers 13:17.
[xlvii] Numbers 13:32-33.
[xlviii] Numbers 14:6-9.
[xlix] Matthew 7:14.
[l] 2 Chronicles 7:14.
[li] Exodus 7:22.
[lii] 2 Thessalonians 2:3.
[liii] Matthew 7:21-23.

www.ingramcontent.com/pod-product-compliance
Lightning Source LLC
LaVergne TN
LVHW021052100526
838202LV00083B/5674